MORGY COAST TO COAST

MORGY COAST TO COAST

by Maggie Lewis
Illustrated by Michael Chesworth

Houghton Mifflin Company
Boston 2005

For Sally and Sam

Thanks to Marilyn Darack, John Kerr,
Tom and Laurie McManus,
Elizabeth Trevithick, and Toph Tucker

Text copyright © 2005 by Maggie Lewis
Illustrations copyright © 2005 by Michael Chesworth

www.houghtonmifflinbooks.com

The text of this book is set in 12.5-point Cheltenham.

Library of Congress Cataloging-in-Publication Data
Lewis, Maggie.
Morgy coast to coast / by Maggie Lewis ; illustrated by Michael Chesworth.
p. cm.
Summary: After moving to Massachusetts and starting fourth grade, Morgy
continues to experience a lot of changes in his life, including learning to play
hockey and the trumpet, and adopting a greyhound named Dante.

ISBN 0-618-44896-9

[1. Family life—Massachusetts—Fiction. 2. Hockey—Fiction.
3. Massachusetts—Fiction.] I. Chesworth, Michael, ill. II. Title.
PZ7.L58726Mo 2005
[Fic]—dc22

2004009471

ISBN-13: 978-0618-44896-8

Manufactured in the United States of America
MP 10 9 8 7 6 5 4 3 2 1

CONTENTS

ONE
Dante to the Rescue

Dear Keith,

For once I'm glad it's the end of summer vacation. Remember when Tory was a baby? Multiply by two. Plus, Savanna. How was soccer camp? Mom lost my hockey camp signup sheet. My friend, that kid Byron, is there. His uncle is a coach. Who's your teacher? Who's goalie?

> *Write,*
>
> *Morgy*

I had to write a book report.

My baby sisters, in their playpen, thought my aunt, Savanna, was playing their favorite game, "run-past-the-door-looking-silly."

Skiff, skiff, skiff, went her googly-eyed purple slippers as she jogged to Mom's room with a blouse on a hanger, to look in the mirror. She was going out to dinner.

"Eeee!" yelled Phoebe, who has curly hair and is actually the serious one. Penelope, who has almost no hair, just cracked up. She loves those slippers. Sometimes Savanna makes them talk to her.

"Book Report," I wrote.

"That blue is great on you," Mom said, "But look, you have paint on the sleeve."

"Oh, drat!" Savanna blew a raspberry kiss to the girls on her way back to her room to find another blouse. Phoebe chuckled. Penelope raspberried back. I looked out the window. The leaves weren't changing color, just getting crisp around the edges, like fried eggs. It was still hot, but it was September. I was going back to school the next day, and so was Savanna. Only she taught art in kindergarten in Los Angeles and I was a student in Puckett Corner, Massachusetts.

"Morgy MacDougal-MacDuff," I wrote. "Mr. Hansom, fourth grade." The assignment sheet came in the mail: "Write a book report as your ticket to fourth grade."

It was the only important thing that hadn't gotten lost. If your mother is a little forgetful and then she has twins, forget it. I felt like we'd been marooned on a desert island all summer. Partly because I was reading *Treasure Island,* partly because all we did all summer was grocery shopping and peekaboo.

Grocery store peekaboo is my sisters' other favorite game. They get so excited that shoppers come from other aisles to see what's the matter. Then Savanna just quietly says, "Aboo," uncovers her face, and pushes the shopping cart along as if nothing happened, which Phoebe and Penelope think is even more of a crackup.

"EEE!!" they said. Savanna was twirling so they could see her swirly purple skirt.

"Perfect," said Mom. Savanna usually went to the movies with Byron's uncle, a firefighter she met when he put out a fire that she started the first time she came to Puckett Corner. But tonight, she was having dinner with a reporter from my dad's paper who was being sent to Paris the next day. Before he went, he said, he had to ask Savanna something very important. "What is he going to ask, do you think?" said Mom.

"Pf," said Savanna, making her "Oh, don't be

silly" noise. "Probably nothing." And she went into Mom's room to put on makeup.

"Eh, eh, eh," said Phoebe, wondering why Savanna didn't go by again. "Waaah," Penelope added. I scooted their playpen around on the bare wood floor. They opened their eyes wide at the ceiling rushing above them. Then I crashed into the window seat, fell down by my book report, and said "Whoa!" They laughed.

Mom came in and picked up Phoebe for her bath. Dad came home and turned on the babies' special tumbling-bear light so Penelope wouldn't get lonely. Then he said, "Let's go put dividers in your binder and sharpen pencils."

We were up in my room when the doorbell rang. High heels clicked downstairs, instead of slippers. Dad went down to give Penelope her bath. Mom nursed Phoebe one more time and sang her a song. Down on the street, a little red car drove away. I closed *Treasure Island*. A dusty smell came out. Even though it was the most boring summer of my life, I felt sad in a comfortable and uncomfortable way. I would miss the book—the pictures, anyway—but it would always be on my shelf. Savanna was going all the way to California, where my old best friend Keith was, and I still missed him.

Pancake sat on my window seat, licked his paw, and closed his eyes in a cat smile.

"You don't have to go to fourth grade," I said.

"Mrah," he agreed, and clawed my window seat cushion gently. I scruffed the stripes on his forehead.

"They've known each other since middle school," Mom was saying when I came in the dining room. "Paris, how romantic. And practical, since she can't cook."

"Well, they can't go out every night on a reporter's salary," Dad said. "Maybe she could take lessons at the Cordon Bleu."

"Or he could get to like toast," said Mom, and she served me some salad.

Was Savanna getting married to this guy and moving to Paris? Then, Keith's and my plan would fall through. I was going to get Mom and Dad to let me stay with Savanna for spring vacation so I could go see my old soccer team and play his computer games. "Plus, how could she be an art teacher in French?" I said.

"It might not be a proposal," said Dad. "He's not

much more grown-up than she is. Good writer, though. The piece he did on rescuing the greyhound got a lot of response."

"Pf," said Mom, and she put croutons in my soup.

"Well?" I said the next morning, the first day of school.

"Great!" said Mom. "You found the shirt that goes with the shorts. I'll get new jeans, soon, I promise. It's on my list. By the way, have you seen my list?" She took a baby bottle and dribbled formula out of it onto Penelope's cereal flakes.

"But is Savanna getting married?" I asked.

"Gee," said Mom, "you'd think she would have told me. The girls woke up when she got home, so she took them for a ride in the car. Have an Awesome, Awesome Aliens Toaster Pastry." Savanna likes to get all the breakfast food you see on TV. Penelope blew a raspberry. Baby cereal fluttered to the kitchen floor, like a tiny, off-white snowstorm.

"Now where did you learn that, young lady?" said Mom. Phoebe, in the next high chair over, chuckled.

When I got home that afternoon, with a project

to do already, the little red car was driving off again. And something was scratching our front door, from the inside. A nose poked open the mail slot.

"Mmm?" it went.

Weird. I thought of ringing the doorbell, but Mom might be taking a nap.

"Snuff-snuff-snuff-snort!" the nose sneezed. It was wet, black, and whiskery, with, right underneath, tiny white teeth between two long white fangs. Pancake! I thought. What if that thing tries to get Pancake? I pushed open the door.

A tall dog pulled his nose back in a hurry. He had big googly eyes like the ones on Savanna's slippers. One of his ears stood up. He had two white toes on his right front paw. The rest of him was black and very thin. Pancake was watching from the landing where the stairs turn a corner, next to a pile of folded baby laundry, Savanna's suitcase, and a bag of dog food. "Pancake?" I said. He looked okay. In fact, he stretched and walked upstairs, like he was saying, "A dog? So?"

"Nnn?" said the dog. I patted his head, which was like patting the seat on a racing bike. He wagged his long, whippy tail, bent his front legs so his bony rear stuck up in the air, and said, "Yark!"

"Hi, Morgo," said Savanna, skiffing downstairs with Phoebe over her shoulder and another suitcase in one hand. "This is what he wanted to ask me. Could I take care of Dante?"

"Eh, eh, eh!" went the baby monitor. Up went Dante's ears.

"There's Penelope," said Savanna. "I guess you'll have to walk him. Sorry, but you also have to pick up the dog-doo. There's a bag on the table. Here's his leash. Don't let go. They can run really fast and they don't know to come back, or did you read the article in the paper?" I wanted to pat Pancake, but Savanna was already jogging upstairs, with Phoebe watching us jouncily over her shoulder and Penelope going "eh, eh" on the monitor. Dante, with his leash on, was nosing through the crack in the door and towing me down the front steps. I left my backpack on the bottom one.

"And, they're off!" yelled Mack out the door of his store, Mack's Corner Spa, as we went by. Dante's ears jogged in time with his footsteps. I kept up. It was kind of like riding a horse. Fun. But I definitely do not like picking up dog-doo. He did it on the grass between the sidewalk and the road, in front of the big fancy house that belongs to Miss Merriweather. "Goodness, have you rescued this

8

elegant, elegant animal?" she said from the porch, where she was having lemonade.

"Rescued?" I said. I needed to be rescued. I already had homework. Plus, Pancake.

"Why, yes, dear. When these dogs finish racing they just put them to sleep, unless they can find a home for them. Horrible. It was in the paper. You're doing a fine thing. There's a garbage can for that, down by the park, and you should knot the bag."

Knotting the bag helped. In the park, Dante saw a squirrel. His head went forward. He tiptoed toward it. The squirrel didn't seem to notice. Dante took a baby step, then another. Then he rushed at it. I was holding the leash, so I did, too. The squirrel ran up a tree. Dante stopped. He looked left. He looked right. He looked at me.

"He's used to chasin' Swifty," said the crossing guard, who was resting on a bench. "Hey, boy." He made kissing noises and patted under Dante's chin. "Swifty, you know?" Dante pointed his eyebrows up at him. "That's what they call mechanical rabbit they chase, at the racetrack. Never did see one go up a tree, did you, boy?" Dante flapped his ears, jogged over to a lilac bush, and lifted his leg on it.

"I guess I better keep walking," I said. The crossing guard stopped a garbage truck. Dante and I crossed. Byron was on his front porch. He ran down the steps.

"Nice dog," he said. "Does this homework kill? We already have a project. I can't believe it. I'm thinking about a pyramid."

"Nile map," I panted. We were jogging behind Dante. Then he stopped and put his head under a hedge to have a better sniff. We ran right into him. He looked up and showed Byron his front teeth and wagged his tail.

"Whoa!" said Byron. "Is he smiling? Where did you get this dog?"

"Savanna —" I started to explain.

"Then he's definitely smiling," said Byron. "Let's take him up to the hill." It's all woods up there, with grass on top. Dante got us to the top in no time. It was still hot. We stopped to get our breath.

You could see the school, Mack's Spa, and the park, a green corner where five roads came together. A girl with long black hair was pushing two little kids on swings.

"Clara Hagopian," Byron explained. "The Hagopians are in the park every day." You could even see Boston, way off in the haze. Dante could see a squirrel. Up went his ears. He started to tip-toe. Then he hustled. Then he galloped, and the leash flew out of my hand. His head went down. His back curved. His feet pounded.

"Dante!" I called. "Here, boy!" But Dante was right on the tail of the squirrel, and he wasn't being fooled by quick turns, either. Then it ran up a tree. Dante stopped a moment, looked around, then jogged down the hill. We followed him, but he went too fast. He blazed out of the trees with his fangs flashing and his leash flying out behind him.

"Help!" said the garbage man, and jumped up on his truck.

"Stop!" yelled the crossing guard as Dante ran into the intersection.

"Oh, no!" said Byron as a fire engine turned on its siren. Cars were everywhere, and trucks, and buses. They all pulled over, but not Dante.

"Yark!" went Dante. Mack looked out the spa door. The Hagopians came to the edge of the park. Miss Merriweather leaned over the rail of her porch. Then the firefighter on the back of the engine leaned down and hooked his arm around Dante's chest. He picked him up. The fire engine flashed, honked, and crossed the intersection. The fireman put Dante back on his feet on the sidewalk in front of us. I took the leash.

"I read in the paper that's the only way to catch a greyhound," he said. "And why didn't you come to hockey camp this summer?" It was Byron's Uncle Mike.

"I wanted to" was all I could say, I was panting so hard. Dante smiled at me.

"Look, he knows you," said Byron.

"You don't see a rescue like that every day," said the Hagopians' grandmother, while Dante stuck one ear up for Clara, who was scratching behind it.

"Thank you so much," I said. I was so glad Dante didn't get hit by a car. "But don't tell my aunt, okay?"

"Your aunt's still here?" said Uncle Mike. "We have to return this dog to Forty-seven Hawthorne Street," he said to the driver. "Get in, boys." We sat on the seat and Dante stood. A taxi was in front of our house. Savanna was dragging a tote bag down the steps. It was full of books and magazines, and, sticking out the top, Penelope's bright pink toy flamingo.

"I thought you were on duty," she said.

"I am," said Uncle Mike, jumping off the end of the fire engine. "I had to bring back this dog and these boys."

"Thank you for the dog and boys, and for this

wonderful summer," Savanna said. Uncle Mike smiled. The fire engine honked. He jumped on and waved all the way around the corner. Savanna waved back. Phoebe and Penelope waved, too. They were just learning how.

"Anyway," Savanna said, hugging my mom and the babies. "Sorry about the dog. You have the number of Give a Hound a Home. Just call and they'll take him back."

"And you." She gave me her usual tight hug full of perfume and curly hair. "I'll miss you the most."

I sniffed, to save up how she smells. I sneezed.

"Take Grammy those pictures," said Mom. "Look, Penelope gave you her toy." Savanna gave the flamingo back to Penelope, who dropped it on the porch and waved again. Savanna got in the taxi, waving and waving. It roared away.

"Puppy dog," said Mom. "Byron. How was your first day of school? There's ginger ale." Puppy dog. I couldn't believe it, but Byron didn't laugh. I guess he thought she meant Dante. We gave Dante water in a mixing bowl and had some ginger ale.

"Look, you can see all his muscles when he drinks," said Byron.

"His ribs, too, poor thing," said Mom, mashing a banana for the girls' dinner.

Byron had to go. I brought in my backpack from the front steps and watched out the little round window by the door. Byron disappeared behind a hedge. Leaves rattled in the wind. Mom took Penelope upstairs to nurse. Dante whined. I put my hand on his bicycle-seat noggin. He pointed his eyebrows up at me. But I guessed somebody else would have to rescue him.

"Wuh, ah," said Phoebe. It was her sad cry. I took her out of the high chair and carried her upstairs. Penelope was crying, too.

"I know, I know," Mom was crooning, in the rocking chair, "Aunt Savanna went home." She put Penelope in the playpen. She took Phoebe. Phoebe was crying too hard to nurse. She put her in the playpen, too. It was that dark, shadowy time of day. I turned on the tumbling-bear lamp, but no one noticed. Mom wound up the music box. You couldn't hear it. "RRRaww!" went both girls. Mom put her head in her hands. Pancake jumped off the window seat and ran up the back stairs to my room on the third floor.

Then Dante jogged by, in a businesslike way, with Penelope's pink flamingo flopping in his mouth.

Penelope stopped crying. "Eh?" said Phoebe. So

15

I threw a toy penguin. Dante ran down the hall after it, skidded, and came back shaking it. He lay down by the playpen with it between his paws. Phoebe sat up and threw a little hippo. Not far, but Dante pounced on it with his ears fluttering. Penelope looked at Phoebe, rolled over, and sat up, too.

"Girls, you sat up," I said, but they were cackling and clapping for Dante.

"Good girls," said Mom. "Good dog. Morgy, did that dog smile at me?"

"Yes, Mom," I said. "We think he smiles."

"Gee," said Mom, "would you believe I've lost the number for that greyhound place already? You better just go downstairs and give him his supper." She was smiling, too.

TWO
Cats and Dogs

Dear Morgy's Dad,
Please pass this on to Morgy. My dad says hi.
Morgy. I can do e-mail. Is this OK? Is this cool?
Also, remember in kindergarten we used to go
to Miss Winthrop's room for fourth-grade bud-
dies? Guess who I have? Miss Winthrop. Raul
is goalie, again.

> *E-mail back!*
> *Keith*

I was in Dad's office reading Keith's e-mail when I heard this sad, whiny noise. I wrote,

We just got a dog, Dante. Later, Morgy and clicked on SEND.

17

Dante was standing at the top of the stairs. His toes were on the top step.

"NNN?" he said.

"Can you walk him?" said Mom, going downstairs with Phoebe. "I guess he came back upstairs, and Dad left early today." When Dad got home last night, he had to carry Dante down to eat his dinner. Racetrack dogs aren't used to stairs, he said.

"Okay. Here, Dante!" Dante looked at the stairs, looked at his toes, backed up, and whined. I called him again. He looked at me. I bent down and slapped my knees. He whined and backed up some more.

"I think he's scared to come down the stairs," I said.

Mom put one arm around his rear and one around his chest. She picked him up, but she tottered. "I might drop him," she said, and put him down. "You'll just have to teach him. Right now; he's gotta go." He licked her face.

I went downstairs and got some bologna. Then I stood on the landing and showed it to him. He put his toes back on the edge of the stairs and pointed his nose at it. But he wouldn't budge. I put the bologna on the third step down and sat next to him. I took one front paw in my hand and put it on the next step down. Then I took the other paw. He didn't want to give it to me, but I put that down a step, too. Then he stretched out, ate the bologna, backed up to the top step, and whined. Mom went by with Penelope in her arms, singing, "Breakfast time for little girls."

"Ppppppp!" said Penelope, holding two handfuls of Mom's hair for balance.

I put the bologna down another step and gave Dante a little push. He plopped one foot, then the other, down a step, got the bologna, backed up, and whined again. Out the window, I saw the crossing guard come out of the spa, put down his coffee on the mailbox, and pull on his white gloves.

I put bologna five steps down, put Dante's feet down two steps, and nudged his rear. He stiffened his legs and rolled his eyes at me. I was still in my pajamas. I went upstairs and got dressed. He waited for me.

"Okay, Dante, let's go, boy!" I said, running to the stairs like it was going to be fun. He ran down the hall with me. I took his collar and started to run down the steps, like, no big deal. He dug in his front paws, my arm jerked back, and his collar came off.

I put his collar back on. I put the bologna back up to the fourth step. He stepped down, leaned way out, and ate it. I gave him a nudge. His muscles got hard and he goggled his eyes at me. "I have to go to school, and you have to go for a walk," I said. He licked my face. Pancake came down the back stairs from my room. He stopped dead and looked at me like, "He's still here?" Then he arched his back like a Halloween cat and went "Rrrrr," low in his throat.

Dante jogged over to sniff him. Pancake fluffed his fur out, made his eyes all big, and went, "rrrrrRRRR!" Dante looked down at him with his ears up.

Pancake batted Dante's nose and hissed. Dante rolled his eyes, backed down the hall, turned, and dived headfirst down the stairs. He crashed going around the corner but got right up, trotted down the last few steps, and said, "Yark!" not very loudly, at the bottom.

Pancake licked his paw like, "No problem," but his eyes were still big and round.

Dante and I ran out of the house and down the front steps, trotted by Mack's, and went up the hill, but not into the woods. Dante did what he had to do. I knotted the bag. High school kids were coming down the hill with us, wearing backpacks, wet hair, and earphones.

When we got home, Mom was squirting a baby bottle onto her wrist. Penelope held her spoon down for Dante to lick. Then he ate Pancake's food. I gave him his own breakfast from the bag the reporter left. I looked for Pancake. He wasn't sunning on the girls' window seat, taking a bath in Dad's armchair, or batting things around on Mom's desk. He was in my room, on top of my bookshelf, with his back hunched up, watching the door.

"Are you okay?" I said. He looked away. I stood on a chair and reached up and patted him, but he didn't purr. "Huh, Pancake?" He looked at me. I scratched under his chin. He batted my hand.

"Can you get down?" I said. He looked out the window with his ears back.

I went to the kitchen and got his bowl and filled it with cat kibbles. I put it on my window seat with a pillow for him to land on. I had to go to school. I put on my backpack. "Take it easy, Pancake," I said. I scruffed the stripes on his forehead. He flicked his ear as if I were a flea.

In math my stomach growled.

"Okay," Mr. Hansom was saying, "who can find another way to get the same answer, which, by the way, is correct?" I felt like I'd never eaten in my whole life. I put my head down on my desk.

"I find this is a better way to see how you're all doing than *diagnostic tests,*" said Mr. Hansom in a warning tone of voice. I sat up.

"Yes, Morgy."

"You could multiply?" I guessed.

"Elaborate," said Mr. Hansom. Elaborate? Mr. Hansom was so hard, no one even made fun of his name. "Morgy? Multiply what by what?"

"The number of doughnuts by the price?" I said.

"Are they all the same price?"

"Oh, right. Multiply the chocolate sprinkles by their price, the powder by their price, the jelly by their price, then add," I said. I was pretty happy to remember all the flavors, but Mr. Hansom frowned.

"You're forgetting the Boy Scout troop."

"I thought this was about doughnuts," I said. My stomach gurgled. Everyone laughed.

"All right, Morgan to the office," said Mr. Hansom. "Maria to the board."

Wow. This guy was hard. I had never been sent to the office. I almost went, once in third grade, when I almost had a fight with this kid Ferguson. I left, with everyone looking at me. It was a long walk. Then, *clop, clop, clop,* I heard the familiar sound of the high heels of Mrs. Caitland, my last year's teacher, catching up with me.

"Did Mr. Hansom send you on an errand?" she said.

"Not exactly," I said.

"Are you not feeling well?" She put her hand on my head. "You look odd."

"I didn't have breakfast," I said, "and I think my cat is mad at me."

"Come with me." She pushed open the door to the teachers' room and a big, sugary, coffee smell flowed out. "Come on," she said, "it's just Miss Vermeil." Miss Vermeil was the music teacher. "Morgy missed breakfast."

"Have a doughnut," said Miss Vermeil. "The brass quintet forgot to come." She pushed a bakery box toward me. "Musicians," she said. "You can finish them." I took a powdered doughnut.

Mrs. Caitland took a cruller. "Your cat is mad at you?" she said. She wasn't trying to make it sound dorky.

"What did you do," said Miss Vermeil, "give it a bath, or get another cat?"

"A greyhound."

"A greyhound." Miss Vermeil raised her eyebrows. "Well, you can see the cat's point, can't you? Oh, honey! Morgy's worried, look at him. I have a cat. You know what they say, they always land on their feet."

I was going to ask her if she thought Pancake would even land on his feet jumping off the bookcase, but the principal's secretary looked around the door and said, "There you are."

"He was hungry!" Mrs. Caitland said.

"I'm sure he was. Come with me." Sometimes if I'm sad and someone's nice to me, I almost cry. But the secretary was so crabby, I didn't. In the principal's office, on the counter, was a large envelope that said, "Morgy!! XXXOOO" in Mom's writing. Inside was an Awesome, Awesome Aliens Toaster Pastry. It was even blackberry-fluff swirl, my favorite flavor. I wondered if Mom knew. That would be cool of her. I got tears in my eyes, but then the secretary said, "Your mother said you left without saying goodbye, but I reminded her that she couldn't come in school with a dog. Besides, she had a stroller, and the elevator is restricted to those in need."

That was good. I didn't want Penelope making

her raspberry noise at Mr. Hansom. I just moved here last year, and I'm still kind of worried about getting laughed at. I finished the toaster pastry and the secretary opened the principal's door so I could go in.

"Sorry to take you out of class," he said. "I'm organizing the lunch and absence reporters. It takes two responsible fourth-graders. You go to each classroom and find out how many lunches and who's absent. This year you and Clara Hagopian were recommended."

The girl with the long black hair was in fourth grade? "Okay," I heard myself say. "Every class?"

"Clara will do half."

I didn't ask him if I was in trouble about the math. I just said, "Okay, I'll do it."

"One more thing," he said. "Have breakfast at home. These first two weeks, I've got all the teachers looking for learning problems. Number one learning problem? Empty stomachs." He made a shooting finger at me.

"Were you in trouble?" said Byron on our way home after school.

"I thought I was," I said. "But I'm supposed to be

a lunch and absence reporter, with Clara Hagopian."

"Oooh," said Byron. "Romance."

"No," I said, wondering if even Byron was going to make fun of me.

Mom was in the kitchen, putting undershirts into a box that said 6 MONTHS, GIRLS. She seemed happy. "They've gone up another size," she said. Also, they were having a good nap.

"Thanks for bringing my breakfast," I said. "Dr. Gazarian wants me to be a lunch and absence reporter. It has to be someone responsible."

"Morgy, that's you!" Mom patted me.

"But Clara's doing it too, and Byron said it was romantic."

Mom said maybe Byron was jealous, which reminded me: "Have you seen Pancake?" I said.

"Napping on your window seat. I made a bed for Dante in the pantry." The bed was Dad's sleeping bag. It had a dent in the shape of Dante, but no Dante. Mom said yes, she had shut the front door. I went up the back stairs. I tiptoed by the girls' room. They were asleep in their cribs with their rears in the air. A soft September breeze blew a baby smell into the hall. He wasn't in Mom and

Dad's room. Up in my room, Pancake ran across my window seat, jumped on my bed, and scuffled up my pillow with all four paws. He let me pat him, but he didn't purr.

I went back down to the girls' room. Something looked odd, in the playpen. It was Dante. He was asleep on his back, with his front paws folded over his chest and his hind legs pushing out the netting. His head was on a teddy bear and he had a little smile on his face. I thought it would be a good idea to just leave him there. But Pancake had followed me. He ran up to the playpen, batted Dante's rump with his paw, and tore off.

"Yark!" Dante flipped over and leaped out of the playpen. It crashed into the wall. Both girls woke up and started to cry.

Dante ran to my stairs. Pancake was three steps up, with his fur fluffed out and his eyes gleaming like new pennies in the darkness. "HNNN," said Dante, settling down on his belly with his paws in front of him and his back knees up like a lion's.

"RRRR!" said Pancake.

"It's okay," I said. I reached out to pat him, but he hissed and ran upstairs.

"No kicking, pumpkin," Mom was saying, at the

28

changing table. "Morgy, do you know how the playpen got way over in the corner, and the mat all scuffed up?"

"Dante jumped out of it when Pancake woke him up."

"What did you say?" Phoebe gurgled and Penelope did her little singing thing. They were getting ready to be fed.

"Dante was asleep in it. Pancake woke him up. He jumped out to chase Pancake."

"Maybe we better rethink this greyhound thing," said Mom.

Dante had his chin on his paws and his eyebrows pointing at me.

"We can't have dog-and-cat fights around the babies," said Mom.

"I'll take him for a walk," I said. Dante stopped at the top of the stairs, goggling his eyes. Then he looked over his shoulder to see if Pancake was around. He dived down, fell in a heap, stood up, and smiled at me.

It's hard to stay sad running down your front steps behind a greyhound. But it's also tough to have everyone smile at the dog you're walking when you might be walking him for the last time, plus your best friend thinks you're being romantic about some responsible fourth-grader. We went past the spa and the park. A different crossing guard got us across the farthest corner. We kept going.

I felt wind in my teeth. Dante's ears were bobbing to his happy prance. His tail was up, curling at the end. He had no idea he might have to go back to the greyhound place. People kept turning to look at him. He must have been a champion racer. He would be re-rescued right away. I felt even worse. We went down a path and before I knew it, Dante was dragging me along the river. He stopped at some stone steps. They led up to a gray house with sunflowers leaning on the front porch. He sniffed the steps by some tiny purple daisies. *Sniff, sniff, sniff,* he went up the steps, pulling me behind. "No," I said. The porch door opened, and out poked another skinny bicycle-seat head. This greyhound was gray, and he was dragging a plump lady with gray hair and red cheeks.

"When did you get him?" she said, as they sniffed each other and started trotting along the river, with me and the lady keeping up.

"Yesterday, but we might have to take him back. He doesn't get along with my cat."

"Doesn't get along, or does he want to eat your cat?" she said.

"I think he just wants to sniff him. But the cat got mad. Mad at me, really. But Pancake, the cat, batted him in the playpen, so Dante jumped out and chased him."

"You're keeping him in a playpen?" Ducks saw us coming and hustled into the river. A small white dog on a footbridge yapped. Dante and the other hound kept going.

"No, he was taking a nap in my sisters' playpen."

"Ah! He misses his crate from the track," she said. "You can get him one. It's like a room of his own, at least till he gets used to your house. Your mom can shut him in there when she goes out and he's alone in the house with the cat. Tell you what. He can use Igor's crate till he settles in. What's your address?"

"Forty-seven Hawthorne," I said.

"I'm just curious. What else does he do? Put his paws on the stove and try to eat your dinner when it's still cooking?"

"No."

"Eat all the toothpaste and throw up?"

"No."

"Get on the couch when you're not looking?"

"No."

"Chew up the telephone?"

"No."

"Pee on the floor?"

"No."

"Igor did all those things, just off the track," she said. "Now he's a perfect gentleman. But it sounds like Dante is one already." We crossed the footbridge and then went over the big bridge that leads back to Puckett Common. "Hawthorne Street is up that way, right?" she said. "I'm Bethany." She shook my hand, then Igor started towing her back down the river path, toward their house. "I'll be over with the crate!" she said as she ran away.

A bunch of geese took off.

THREE
What's So Funny About Lunch?

Hey, Morgy,
A dog? What about your cat?
Keith

Mr. Hansom believed in homework. One night we got a whole sheet of story problems. Boy Scouts were selling more doughnuts, people were paddling canoes upriver and downriver, and a girl was in trouble at the zoo. But it wasn't about them. It was about adding, subtracting, multiplying, and dividing. At the bottom it said, "If you think I'm being sneaky, you're right. Hint: In number three, the answer has something to do with the length of the rope. C. Hansom."

Pancake jumped off the top of my bookcase and

curled up on my desk with his fur overlapping the worksheet. He mostly stayed in my room now, since Dante was too scared to go up the dark, narrow back stairs. He started a cat bath and knocked my binder on the floor. "Why is it the rope and not the lion or the bowl of milk?" I said. He stopped in the middle of licking his belly fur, with his tongue half sticking out. Then he purred and started up his bath again, as if he'd suddenly remembered that cats don't have homework.

I didn't get it. I wondered if Byron did. But I hadn't talked to him yet this week. Monday, when I read the lunch menu for the first time, everyone laughed, and he did, too. Well, he smiled. Then he didn't wait for me after school. He wasn't at Mack's either. Or today, Tuesday. Then math took so long, it was already dark.

The leaves on the old maple tree in front of our house looked like lanterns in the street light. Mom was singing to the girls in their bath. Dad came home and Dante thumped his tail against his crate. Pancake bit the eraser of my pencil. You can still be lonely in a full house.

"How's Byron?" Mom asked at dinner.

I shrugged.

"Is he sick?" said Dad.

"No," I said. Maybe Byron thought I was mad that he laughed and didn't wait for me. I wasn't, though.

"Then are you sick?" Dad said.

"No," I said. "Everyone laughs at me when I read the lunch menu."

"What's so funny about lunch?" said Dad.

"It's gross." I didn't even want to talk about it.

"What was the menu?" said Dad.

"Gobbly Turkey Pies with Cauliflowerettes in Sauce with a Flaky Crust was on Monday," I said. "Today was Fall Corny-Copia with Chips." I knew them by heart. I had to do nine classrooms.

"Better to laugh than cry," said Dad.

Mom said Dr. Gazarian should read the lunch menus over the PA system. She would suggest it when she and Byron's mom went to see him about the Winter Fair.

"Don't, okay?" I said. I thought the kids in my class would figure out I was scared to read the menu, and laugh even more.

Wednesday was Crisp Fish Sticks and Puckett Fries, with Peas. I don't know why they laughed at that. I might have said "fried pucks." Being laughed at was reminding me of when I was new last year, and I worried about hockey all the time.

Well, I was still worried about hockey. Tryouts were tomorrow. And about Byron. I didn't see him after school, again. Maybe he was just being nice before and he wasn't actually my friend. He was nice to everyone.

Dante was my friend, anyway. He was starting to wag his tail instead of just standing around looking at me. When Bethany brought over Igor's crate, she also gave me a special mitten with little rubber bristles so I could brush him. A regular brush would hurt, she said, because his fur was short. Now he was getting shiny.

When he heard me take the leash off the hook in the hall, he ran down the stairs with his hind legs trying to pass his front ones. He skidded the hall rug into a pile, came to a stop, and smiled. He was so cool.

I clipped on the leash and we ran to the river. Bethany and Igor weren't down there. We passed the ducks and went over the footbridge. As we walked over Puckett Corner Bridge back to the common, a van beeped. Mrs. Noonan, Byron's mom, said, "Want a ride?"

"Thanks, but he needs his walk," I said.

"Okay. Did Byron tell me Mr. Hansom gave you a project?"

"Pyramids," I said.

"I think Byron's a little lost. Could you work with him on it, if you don't have a partner? Or just give him a call anyway. That'll cheer him up."

Cheer him up? He's a good hockey player and no one laughs at him, I thought later as I stood in the back pantry, watching Dante eat. The phone rang. Mom handed it to me.

"The pyramid," said Byron.

"Due Friday," I said. "I have this square cereal we could use."

"I'll be right over."

We used a piece of a moving box for the base. We got Dad's T-square and drew a perfect square. We glued on Tiger Paw Power Wheats. Dante came and lay on his cushion in Igor's crate. Mom kept it in the dining room so he could get the morning sun.

The second row of Wheats wobbled. I thought we should glue them on top of each other. But Byron said then the pyramid would have straight up-and-down sides, like an apartment building. I thought of sticking in toothpicks, at a slant, to hold them up. That worked. We ran out of toothpicks, so we went to Mack's and got another box, also some candy bars for us. We got to the top. It looked more like a haystack with corners than like a pyramid. I guess Byron thought so too, because he didn't smile, even when Dad got home, turned on the dining room light, and said, "Aha! Egyptian slaves."

It was dark outside. Dante was asleep in his crate with his chin on his paws and his toes twitching. "Man," said Byron, "I better go. Tomorrow."

"We also have to write about how we did this."

"If we finish." Byron was all serious. Maybe he was having a hard school year, too. "We have hockey tryouts tomorrow night, and this is due Friday," he said.

"That's okay," said Dad. "See what you can get done tomorrow after school, then after hockey, come over for dinner and you boys can use my computer."

"Okay," said Byron. Then he left.

"Are you trying out for hockey?" said Dad at dinner.

I shrugged. It was fun sometimes. But I wasn't looking forward to practicing with the seven-and-unders again. Last year was my first year playing hockey, so they put me with little kids. Now that I was almost ten and in fourth grade, maybe I could skate with the third-graders. I wasn't as good as a fourth-grader yet. Even the third-graders probably went to hockey camp. I put my head down on the table next to my soup.

"Aw, they laughed at him about the lunch menu again," said Mom.

"Eh, eh, eh, huh-wah!" said Penelope on the baby monitor. Mom ran upstairs.

"Do they laugh at the other kid?" said Dad.

"Clara? No," I said. I watched her once. She was good. She kept her chin down and frowned, with her long black hair swinging forward. You would never laugh at her.

"James?" said Mom in the baby monitor, "could you bring up two bottles?"

"Talk to Carla," said Dad, going out to the kitchen.

"Clara," I said.

"Wuh, ah," said Phoebe on the monitor.

I asked Clara the next day.

"What's so funny about lunch?" she said.

"Piping Hot Cheeseburger Pockets, Chips, and Crisp Carrot Sticks, or Sealed-With-A-Kiss Bag Lunch with Real Chocolate Kiss Inside?" I said.

"It just says SWAK," she said. "Just read it, like, 'swack.' They know what it is."

"Okay," I said.

"Swack" worked fine till I got to my own class. I had the stomachache I used to get in hockey last year before this big kid, Ferguson, would knock me over. "May I have your attention please?" I said. "The hot lunch for today is Pooping Hot Cheeseburger Pockets, Chips, and Crisp Carrot Sticks. I mean, Piping Hot. Piping."

I didn't even get to the part about the chocolate kiss, they were laughing so loud. How could I say "pooping" in front of the whole class?

Even Mr. Hansom looked surprised. I was blushing. Byron was blushing. What on earth was a hot cheeseburger pocket, anyway?

"All right, class," said Mr. Hansom. "It was a tongue twister. Settle down."

"How many want hot lunch?" was all I could say.

"Pooping hot," said Byron, who came out the back door with me after school.

"Well, at least you didn't laugh," I said.

"I never laugh," said Byron.

"You did the first day, remember, Gobbly Turkey Pies?"

"I was happy," said Byron. "I love Gobbly Turkey Pies."

I didn't say anything, because what if he did? He came home with me so we'd have time to paint the River Nile flowing past our pyramid before hockey.

First, Dante needed his walk. He raced downstairs, skidded all the way to Byron on the hall rug, and smiled. "Cool, cool dog," said Byron. Dante towed us to the river. It was a warm, windy day. He was sniffing the air. Leaves rained down, tiny yellow ones, brown ones as big as notebook paper, and bright red curly ones like breakfast cereal. Byron didn't talk. I was just going to ask him if he was mad at me when a sleek gray head poked between us. It was Igor, catching up with Dante.

"Whoa!" said Byron.

"Well, Morgy," said Bethany, at the other end of the leash, "you didn't tell me you knew Byron. By, we're all awful proud of your uncle and I'm sure he'll be just fine."

"What happened?"

"Byron's Uncle Mike just finished forest fire training. Now he's going out to the Crestwood fire in California with a crew from New Hampshire." Byron frowned toward the footbridge. "We miss him almost as much as you over at Youth Services," she said gently, "but Mrs. Almonio is going to give it a good try with the hockey. You going tonight? Be nice to her." Byron didn't say anything. We kept going. The ducks hustled into the river. Bethany and Igor went back over the footbridge.

"He was going to move up to the ten-and-unders this year," said Byron as we crossed Puckett Common.

"He'll be okay, though, right?" I said.

"He's trained," Byron said, and shrugged.

We painted on the Nile and had a snack. Byron's mom picked us up for hockey tryouts. The rink was cold as winter, and dark. I got a cold feeling in my stomach, like last year. I fell down in the beginning, which is just skating-around time, without Ferguson even knocking me down. When Mrs. Almonio came out on the ice, wearing sneakers, fuzzy red mittens, and matching earmuffs, I sat with the little kids from last year, but she called my name with the fourth-graders. I fell down skating over to them. The little kids cheered. I did okay in tryouts. I still did the T-stop while everyone else stopped with a sharp turn and ice spray, but I could go straight pretty fast. I fell a couple of times skating around the cones. But no one fell on me.

"I'll call you about team assignments," Mrs. Almonio said.

"Hey, better," said Byron when we changed out of our skates.

After dinner, the Nile was dry. We turned on Dad's computer and wrote "How We Made Our Pyramid." It still looked bad. Mom found some gold spray paint. "I made a Christmas wreath with that same cereal once," she said. "It looks much better gold."

"I don't know," said Byron, frowning.

"They were made of stone, Mom," I said.

"I'll just do the back," she said. This was bad. Your parents weren't supposed to help. Byron and I looked at each other.

"Huh," said Byron, when she turned the pyramid around for us to see.

"You think about it. I have to check on the girls," she said.

Byron didn't say anything. Dad looked at the pyramid and said, "Let's have some brownies," and went in the kitchen.

"It'll be okay," I said, although it wouldn't.

Byron thought I meant the Crestwood fire would be okay. He said the firefighters have compasses and two-way radios and Pulaski trenching tools to dig firebreaks, and portable shelters in case they get caught in a "burn over," which is if they're surrounded by fire. He said he got to help Uncle Mike pack, and that's why he wasn't there after school. Then he buttoned up his lower lip and frowned.

"I'm sorry," I said.

"It's okay," he said. "It sort of looks like a pyramid."

"No, I mean, sorry you're worried."

"I just wish he could be my coach. Then I feel bad because it's so selfish. I should wish that he puts the fire out and, you know, survives."

"I feel bad because he was my coach last year, and I can't even play," I said.

"Don't. He loves it when you can't do something and he teaches you. He taught me to skate."

"Cool."

"I even have his old skates."

We went back in the dining room. Mom had sprayed the whole pyramid gold. "Gee," she said, "I thought it would look better."

"No, it's fine," said Byron. "I mean, thanks, I didn't even feel like doing it at all."

"Aww," Mom said, and patted his sticking-up black hair. Don't, I thought. He might cry. He didn't, though. They let me walk him home, even though it was after ten. We had Dante. It was raining. Byron didn't say anything, so I didn't either.

"Thanks," he said from the top of his porch stairs.

We waved. I felt bad, but only because he was my friend.

When we got back, Dante got a drink of water, then went back to his crate to sleep. Pancake was sitting on top of it. Dante smelled him. He smelled Dante. Then they both curled up, Pancake on top and Dante inside, as if they were in a bunk bed.

> Dear Keith,
> Don't worry about Pancake, he's cool. Where's Crestwood? Because my friend, that kid Byron's, uncle is fighting that fire. Hope you are OK out there. Fine here,
>
> Morgy

I clicked on SEND. Before I went to bed, I looked at the lunch menu on the fridge. Friday I would have to say "Buttons 'n' Bows Tuna Casserole with Olives." But even that didn't seem so serious anymore.

FOUR
Trumpet Volunteer

Hey, Morgy,
How's your friend's uncle? We can even see
smoke down here. It's dark, and the sun is, like,
orange. Did you get on a team? We're going to
the playoffs. Wish you could come. See you,
                                    Keith

We got a B minus on our project. Mr. Hansom
wrote "Pyramids were not gold, although the
Pharaohs would have appreciated the thought."

I got on the ten-and-under hockey team. Dad
looked so happy, I didn't tell him Mrs. Almonio
probably didn't know enough to put me with the
little kids. Our first game was in two weeks. I was
actually playing, I guessed. Or maybe Uncle Mike

would be back by then and put me with the third-graders.

Practice wasn't scary. We did the same kind of drills I did with the little kids, skate to the middle of the rink and stop, skate backwards back. Or the opposite. The other ten-and-unders were mad. They wanted to scrimmage and practice shooting. I just wanted to stay standing up. We stood around a lot while Mrs. Almonio told different kids to show us backward skating and which way to turn.

"Like we don't know," someone said. Then this kid Ryan hooked his stick around Danny's skate. Danny fell over. Danny's friends pushed Ryan. Ryan started laughing and fell on Danny, then Danny's friends fell on Ryan.

Mrs. Almonio asked what on earth was going on and took all our hockey sticks away for the rest of practice. We skated in circles, lines, and smaller circles. We turned, stopped, and went backwards. She gave back the sticks at the end, but by then the next team was on the ice and we had to leave.

"Come back, Uncle Mike," Byron said to himself while he took off his skates. He sounded sad. Uncle Mike called Aunt Mary once when he landed in California, and once on Monday on another fire-fighter's cell phone. But it was Thursday. Byron said, "Aunt Mary's worried. He's her favorite great-nephew. She always says that, even in front of Dad." Aunt Mary always watched out for Byron, his big brother, Tom, his little sister, Polly, and sometimes even me. I said I thought she would be especially good at watching over her favorite great-nephew. But Byron said Uncle Mike was all the way in California, in a fire, without even a phone number, and you couldn't tell much from the news. That was hard even for Aunt Mary to watch over.

Dad picked us up from hockey. At home, Mom and Byron's mom were working on a plan to raise money for a slide for the school playground. At least, they called it a playground. There was a swing set they put in last year, a tree, a hill, and a sidewalk. They were sitting at our kitchen table. It was covered with little things to sell at the Winter Fair: snowmen made of pompoms, a little skier made of a pinch clothespin and a regular one, and clown refrigerator magnets, also Mrs. Noonan's cell phone.

"Any news?" said Byron.

Byron's mom shook her head. "The fire got worse, and you know he'll be right there, helping out, so we won't hear for a while." She was smoothing Byron's hair, which kept sticking back up again. "Bunny rabbit," she said, "he's had all that training, he'll be okay." I was thinking, Bunny rabbit? No wonder he never laughs at me.

"Let us know when he calls," Mom said as Byron and his mom got ready to go home.

"We will, and meantime we need your prayers," said Mrs. Noonan, pushing Byron out the door. Mom swept the snowmen, clowns, and skiers, which were all smiling, into her knitting bag. She sniffed. "We might not hear right away, but you can pray right now. That way you'll be ready to help Byron, whatever happens."

I said, "Byron has Uncle Mike's skates."

"Aw," said Mom, and she blinked. The baby monitor made a noise. Dante came in with a ball of fluffy, sparkly, light blue yarn in his mouth. Mom unwound it from his nose and ran upstairs, wiping her eyes with it. "Here I come, girls." Her voice wobbled.

Dante smiled at me. "Good dog," I said. We took a walk. It was dark. Uncle Mike didn't need me to cry. I thought how he liked it if you didn't know something, so he could teach you. I had a feeling that, right then, if he was in any kind of trouble, he could learn what he needed to know.

I gave Dante his dinner. Dad came home. The girls had dinner with us. Penelope put her hands in her baby carrots, then wiped them on her almost-no hair and dried them on the curtains. Mom didn't even get mad. She wiped the curtains with a clean cloth diaper, turned it over and wiped the top of Penelope's head, folded it again and wiped her hands.

I stayed up with Mom and Dad to watch the ten o'clock news. There were some scenes of the Crestwood fire, the worst in a hundred years, they said. I looked for the firefighters. Then I saw tiny black trees in the bottom of the flames. Those flames were so big, you wouldn't even see the firefighters.

After they said good night, I got up and went to the attic part of the third floor, at the other end from my room. I looked out the round window under the peak of the roof. I could just see Aunt Mary's window, under its own little roof like an eye under a surprised eyebrow. The light was on. Maybe Uncle Mike was calling her. The next morning, the light was off and Aunt Mary was marching across the park toward the church. In school, when kids asked Byron about Mike he just shook his head. So I didn't ask.

That was the day the brass quintet came. I wondered if Miss Vermeil had gotten them another box of doughnuts. I sat next to Byron in assembly.

"I'm happy to present Boston Baked Brass, at long last," she said. "They'll play for you, then you can ask questions. Band has already started for this year, but if you get inspired and want to play something, talk to me or Mr. Profundo and we'll give you a permission form to take home."

I wasn't paying attention. I was thinking about the fire and Uncle Mike, how Byron must miss him since we couldn't even use sticks in hockey, and whether or not I even liked hockey. Four men in black suits and one woman with long red hair and a shiny, curving French horn were sitting on chairs behind music stands. The kids sat on the floor with the cafeteria tables folded up around the walls. Some fifth-graders were fighting. Two girls in front of me were braiding another girl's hair. A teacher frowned at them. Another teacher hauled a different fifth-grader out in the hall.

The musicians didn't seem to mind, or even notice. I could just see their eyebrows over their music stands. They looked happy and interested. A blare of music curled right up to the cafeteria ceiling. It cut through the smell of Ritzy Chicken and Broccoli Surprise. It was like a beam of sunlight.

"Whoa," I whispered, and hit Byron's arm, forgetting not to bother him.

But Byron looked as happy and interested as the brass quintet. Everyone was clapping. He slowly stood up, to see the instruments better. Everyone else stood up, too.

"Ooh, a standing ovation," said Miss Vermeil. "That was by Purcell."

"Let's play trumpets," I said to Byron. I don't think he heard me, he was clapping so loud. Then it was time to go back to our classrooms. I saw Miss Vermeil at the door. She said, "So how's the cat?"

"I think they're friends," I said, and took two forms. I wanted to give one to Byron on the way home, but he was just quiet. It was like he was listening for Uncle Mike to call.

"Can Byron and I take trumpet lessons at school?" I said to Mom, who was changing Phoebe. Penelope was on her happy whale rug on her hands and knees, rocking. She took a couple of crawling steps forward, landed on her face, and sat down, then reached up and went, "Wah!" I picked her up and got a little cereal out of her hair. She tried to turn around in my arms. She wanted to get down and try again. "She was crawling, Mom," I said.

"Baby gates," said Mom.

"So, do you think Byron and I could take trumpet?" I read her the form: "Lessons are free, and the instrument rental, from the reputable firm of Harrington School Music, is thirty-five dollars a year, including insurance." Penelope tried again. She was off the rug. She sat down and started up again. She crawled around the corner. Pancake sniffed her, then headed downstairs. She reached for his tail.

"Morgy, get her before she gets to the stairs," said Mom. I did, but she wiggled to get loose. Mom put Phoebe in her fuzzy suit. "We're going to the hardware store. Come on. They love to go in the stroller when Dante comes." Phoebe's fuzzy suit was purple, with cat faces."Look at that, they've almost grown out of them and it's just the beginning of November," said Mom, trying to do a snap on Penelope's kicking foot in blue, with stars.

The man in the hardware store let Dante come in, but Dante whined because there was no place to lie down. I walked him around the common while Mom decided on a baby gate. I saw Mrs. Noonan go by and waved. She didn't wave back. She was concentrating on traffic, or listening for her cell phone. I thought of how high those flames went. But then I remembered about Uncle Mike learning what he needed to know. When he put out the fire at our house, he said it was a blessing the roof didn't catch. I thought he could find a blessing out there, too.

The stroller lurched out of the hardware store with two big boxes tied to the handles and Mom pushing. She handed me a plastic bag. "When we get home, you can plug these things into all the empty sockets," she said. Dante and I ran ahead. Penelope yelled, so Mom ran after us. *Thump, thump, thump,* went the boxes. Phoebe clapped.

When Dad got home, he got out his toolbox and put up the baby gates, one for the girls' room and one for the back stairs. Mom gave the girls their bath after dinner, because now Phoebe wiped her hands in her hair, too. It said "Parent or Guardian signature" on the bottom of the forms. Dad was working at his desk. I asked him if Byron and I could play the trumpet.

"What does Mrs. Noonan say?"

"I think she's a little worried, so I didn't ask. I

thought you could sign and they could pay you back. It's thirty-five dollars."

Dad thought that would be okay, if we practiced in the attic. "But what if Byron doesn't like it? The Noonans will owe us thirty-five dollars for nothing."

I told him about Byron standing up and clapping. "It's cool. They played 'Trumpet Volunteer.'"

"'Trumpet Voluntary,' probably," said Dad, and he smiled. "Give me that," he said, and he signed one form. While he was writing the check, he said he wondered how we would practice and play hockey, too. I said we could. Dad wrote a note on Byron's form, put the forms and check in an envelope, and gave the envelope to me.

"Yes!" I said.

"'Yes,' he says," said Dad to Dante, and took him for his bedtime walk.

The next day I gave the envelope to Mr. Hansom. On Monday, Miss Vermeil, on the PA, said Byron and I should go to the cafeteria.

Byron looked surprised. We walked down the hall together. I didn't want to tell him. Playing trumpets suddenly didn't seem like such a good idea. Plus, we had gotten in the habit of walking along not talking, because of Uncle Mike. But I

had to say something. The cafeteria doors were coming up.

"I signed us up to play trumpet," I said.

Byron just looked at me.

"Was that okay?"

"No," he said.

Wow, this was all he needed, on top of an uncle in danger and Mrs. Almonio for hockey. I felt so bad, I couldn't even say I was sorry. We walked into the cafeteria.

"Here comes our brass section," said Miss Vermeil. "Boy, am I glad you guys signed up!" Our trumpets were on a table, leaning on their black cases. Byron didn't say a thing. He reached out and took his shining trumpet.

"Do this," said Miss Vermeil, and blew a raspberry like Penelope, only drier. I made the noise and looked at the mouthpiece.

Byron just put his trumpet to his lips and trumpeted.

"Wow," said Miss Vermeil, "not everyone can do that the first time."

"BRAAA!" trumpeted Byron. "BRAAA!"

"Excellent," said Miss Vermeil with her hands over her ears.

FIVE
Puckett Corner Pumas

Dear Keith,

Do you still see smoke? Because Byron's uncle called and said it's contained. We're playing trumpets. Good luck in the playoffs. We have a hockey game Saturday. I might have to play, help!

Morgy

Byron called me Sunday night. Uncle Mike was okay. "But guess what? There's another fire, over by Nevada."

"Does he have to put that one out too?"

"He wants to. The other guys on his crew are all going."

"When does he get back?"

"Probably not in time for the game. Oh, yeah, he said chin up to the team, and way to go, Morgy."

"Way to go? That I'm on the team?" Uncle Mike thought about me during a huge, record, hundred-year fire in California? That made me feel worse. Mrs. Almonio was letting us use our sticks again, but we still hadn't scrimmaged. Everyone came early and shot goals during skating-around time. I wasn't even sure I knew the rules.

On Monday Ryan said, "This is ice dancing!" and had to sit in the penalty box.

Wednesday, Mrs. Almonio gave us positions and schedules. Ryan was goalie. Byron was center forward, and I was in back, in the middle, almost exactly where I used to be in soccer, in California. Byron and I stayed out on the ice after practice, to whack pucks at Ryan. We should have gone to the locker room because our time was up, but Ryan kept asking for one more.

Suddenly, a stick hooked around my skate. I started to fall, but I lifted my foot over it, turned around, and yelled, "Cut it out, Ferguson!" I knew it was Ferguson, because that was how he made me fall down all last winter.

"What?" he said.

"Get out of here, Ferguson," said Byron.

"You get out," said Ferguson. "We've got the ice now. And good luck on Saturday. My brother's coaching the Winston Wildcats this year."

"Who are the Winston Wildcats?" I said in the locker room.

"Who are we?" said Byron, sadly undoing his skates.

"Here are your jerseys; sorry they're late," said Mrs. Almonio on Friday. "We're the Puckett Corner Pumas. And we have a new teammate. This is Clara Hagopian. Please make her feel welcome."

Clara shook back her hair, put on her helmet, and skated over to me, frowning as if she were about to read the SWAK lunch menu.

"Clara," I said, "welcome." She put in her mouth guard and nodded. I tried to think how to pay her back for helping me with lunch, but she skated off too fast. At the end of practice, when everyone shot goals at Ryan, all of Clara's went in.

"Phew," said Byron after practice, unlacing his skates. "I guess Uncle Mike called someone."

"From a fire, over by Nevada?"

"I asked him to. I wanted him to get Haig

Hagopian, but I guess he didn't hear me. She'll be good, though. Your girlfriend."

"No," I said. I hated that.

The game was at nine on Saturday morning, in Winston.

"Winston, Massachusetts?" Mom said.

"Wow," said Dad, looking at a map while we had breakfast. "You're going almost all the way to Rhode Island."

"Here, puppy dog," said Mom, "take a snack." She gave me two teething crackers in a sandwich bag.

"That's not very much," said Dad, so she put in some raisins. Dad gave me money for lunch. The Noonans' van came up our driveway and honked. I picked up my sports bag and stick. Phoebe, sitting in her high chair, did her new trick, tilting her head to one side so I would tilt my head to one side.

Penelope waved her spoon, which flew out of her banana-covered hand. Dante clomped it and took it into the hall to lick. Pancake was curled up tight in some sun he found on the newspaper pile in the back pantry. Walking out the door, I felt homesick.

An almost-winter wind went up my pant legs on

the way down the back steps. "There he is!" said Mr. Noonan. The big square black van was dark and warm. It smelled of sneakers and popcorn. Snow started flying past the windows as we drove. Mr. Noonan said he didn't think it would stick. He plowed snow for the town of Puckett Corner. "Anyway, they'll beep me if it gets bad."

I was hoping it would and we'd have to turn back. I fell asleep. The door sliding open woke me up. Snowflakes blew in. It wasn't sticking, it was just running around the parking lot. We got dressed in the locker room, filled our water bottles, and sat down on the bench out in the rink. Clara sat between us.

"Hey, Clara," said Byron. Clara's grandmother, behind us in the stands, handed Clara a handkerchief. She put it up the sleeve of a purple leotard she had on under her jersey. "So Ferguson's big brother is their coach?" she said.

"Yeah," said Byron. "Not Mickey—the really big one, Daniel."

"The one who burned down the ball shed," said Clara.

"They used to have a ball shed at school, for recess," Byron explained. "That was Uncle Mike's first fire. Look, there's Daniel."

A tall fat guy with light brown hair that stuck up between two bald spots, kind of like a baby's hair, sat down with his team and reached over to shake hands with Mrs. Almonio. She had a band around her wrist with a pincushion on it, with needles and thread sticking out. Her hand disappeared into his, and she smiled politely. She did not look like a hockey coach.

"Morgy," said Mr. Noonan from behind me, "if she puts you in, just watch the other defenseman. Be fine." He patted me on the shoulder pad.

Before I could tell Mr. Noonan not to worry because I had told Mrs. Almonio I had never played in a game, she pointed to me and Stan.

"There you go," said Mr. Noonan. Easy for him to say, I thought, as I put my skates on the ice and slid away from the bench. First we warmed up Ryan by hitting pucks at him. Then it was time to start. It got quiet for a long cold moment.

Byron, Clara, and Anthony were in front. I knew not to be afraid. I knew it didn't hurt to fall down. But the Winston Wildcats looked like a bunch of Fergusons, ready to knock me over and laugh. I was afraid.

"Stay still during the face-off," Mr. Noonan called. I was trembling all over from the cold of the rink and the cold in my stomach. The referee smacked down the puck, Byron and the other center hacked at it, and it flew past me. Stan zoomed over and whapped it away from our goal. "Now we can move," he said as he went by.

These guys didn't skate like the seven-and-unders, who just run with their blades going *chop, chop, chop*. These guys swooped, fast. I stayed near Stan. I got in his way. "You don't have to say 'sorry' every time," he said.

First, Clara hit the puck way down toward the Wildcats' goal and hurried after it with Byron and Anthony. I thought they'd be down there awhile, but the goalie hit it right at me. The Wildcats, with their blades glinting like barracudas and their sticks clacking, came after it. Stan stepped in and whacked it to Byron. He almost made a goal but the Wildcats got it again. Back they came, clattering and glinting. This time the puck was right by my skates. They were all around me. I tried to back up. I fell. Stan reached over and hit the puck. It disappeared among Wildcat blades, but Byron snagged it and made a goal.

"Okay, Byron!" said his dad.

"Here's how to skate backwards," said Clara quietly while everyone cheered about the goal. She moved her feet apart and together, like a seal swishing its fins. I said I could do that, but when I tried, I fell down again. They waited till I got up for the face-off.

Even though Byron hit it way down to the Wildcats' goal, the puck was heading for me in no time. Here it came. I skated backwards, right past it. It got by Ryan and hopped in the goal. Ferguson's brother said, "Yes!"

My face got hot. "Sorry," I said. I thought of apologizing for apologizing, but that would have been worse.

Then after the face-off the Wildcats zoomed the puck behind the goal and hooked it in from there. The period ended, and we had water. Mr. Noonan squirted Ryan with his water bottle so he didn't have to take off his mask.

"Okay?" said Mr. Noonan. Ryan nodded. "Tough team, guys," Mr. Noonan said to us. "You're goin' good. Mrs. Almonio and I will tell that to Mike Noonan." He gave a thumbs up and people clapped.

"I certainly couldn't do what you're doing," added Mrs. Almonio, "Kyril and Don, go in for MacDougal and Stan." She looked at us and then down at her clipboard, just to make sure. For hockey, they just call me MacDougal. I sat on the bench and watched, to figure out what to do if I had to go in again. Kyril was little. He could skate forward and backwards. When a Wildcat skated right at him, he just went sideways. He stayed crouched down, didn't fall, didn't skate past the puck but scooted it to Byron. He did everything right, the opposite of me. Byron almost made another goal.

Mrs. Almonio and Clara's grandmother sewed red stripes on blue jeans for a show called *Babes in Toyland* that they were doing at Youth Services. Clara's grandmother wondered who was the best singer: Michaela Fahey or Michaela Ortiz? Mrs. Almonio hoped Maria's mother would sell snow-flake cookies at intermission. Stan probably wished I wasn't in his line. That's what I was wishing, too. The Wildcats didn't hit the puck to Kyril nearly as much as to me. Duh, I thought, they hit it to me because then it goes right past me, into the goal.

Mr. Noonan leaned over and said in my ear, "Remember what Mike told you last year. Be fine."

The third period started. The Wildcats were winning, 5 to 3. Kyril and Don came in the gate to the bench. Stan climbed over the partition and onto the ice. I climbed after him. I didn't fall. Then I did fall. A Wildcat was skating away. He smiled over his shoulder. I was mad. I wondered if Ferguson told his brother to tell the Wildcats how easy it was to knock me over.

I got up. That's what Uncle Mike said last year. "Get up, hustle, and dig in." Another Wildcat went by, close. I felt stupid. I hoped Uncle Mike really did like it if you didn't know stuff. Because he had to teach me a lot, last year. Then he gets in some big fire and can't even coach his nephew, who's actually good. Then the puck was right by my skates, with a stick reaching for it. It was the stick of the Wildcat who blew by me, smiling at me like he didn't even have to push me over. Wildcats were all around me. But I was just on ice, not in an emergency. I was surrounded by kids with sticks, not flames, and Uncle Mike would even be okay surrounded by flames, I just knew.

"Dig in" was what he used to say. So I didn't look at them, I looked at the puck. I hit it to Clara. She did this cool, fast turn and shot it straight into Byron's stick with Wildcats clattering after it.

Byron clacked it at the goal. The goalie shot it out, all the way back to me. I hit it to Clara again.

I thought that was cool of me, but then I couldn't even see Clara for a minute, there were so many Wildcats around her. Then out came the puck, back to me. I was leaning on the wrong skate. I almost fell over. I stuck my stick out to hold myself up. It didn't work. I fell on my stick. My stick hit the puck. I hit the ice. Wildcats laughed. Puckett Corner Pumas even laughed. Byron didn't laugh. He made a goal.

"Yes!" said Stan. Byron jumped on me before I could get back up. The rest of the Pumas jumped on him. That was another thing Uncle Mike said: get right up. Then Byron made another goal. The buzzer went. It was a tie.

"Nice teamwork, Clara, Byron, and"—Mrs. Almonio checked her clipboard—"MacDougal." She patted my cheek. Everyone laughed, but Mr. Noonan shook his head.

"Thank you, Mrs. Almonio," I said, and shook hands with her.

"Morgy, hey, an assist," said Mr. Noonan as we had hamburgers on the way home.

"They were just distracted by Clara," I said.

"There you go," he said, like that was my plan.

"Clara's good," I said.

"Getting there," said Byron. He didn't say "your girlfriend." The hamburgers tasted great. My stomach was finally warming up, and the game didn't even last that long. But I still couldn't wait till Uncle Mike came back.

SIX
It's Thanksgiving

Hey, Morgy,

You're right, no more smoke out here. We have to play Oxnard again. Maybe when you come out, you could practice with us, if you live through hockey! Ha! Guess what, I'm playing trumpet, too. Really.

Keith

It was the day before Thanksgiving.

"This is good," said Byron. We were missing Mr. Hansom's Math Teaser Turkey Shoot. The music room was full of November sun. It had windows to the ceiling and you could see the whole hill, with all the houses lined up like toys.

72

"Excellent," I agreed.

"Let's see if we can blow an A," said Mr. Profundo. He talked with his mouthpiece by his lips so he could trumpet right after he talked. "Braaah!" we went. Byron could make it really loud.

"Nice," he said. "Good, Morgy. Again?"

"Braahhhh!"

"Okay, let's try our tune!"

It sounded like car horns playing "God Rest Ye Merry, Gentlemen." The band was playing at the Puckett Corner Senior Center before Christmas vacation, and they needed trumpets, which was why we got out of math.

"That's what I'm talking about. Okay." Mr. Profundo pointed his trumpet at me and nodded, and we started again. He took Byron's trumpet and put a little valve oil on it. "Blow me an A," he said to Byron. "Okay, better." By the time the bell rang, we had gotten through "let nothing you dismay."

"Happy Thanksgiving! Maybe you could practice?" he yelled down the hall after us.

I was happy. Byron, his sister, Polly, and his brother, Tom, were coming to my house because Mrs. Noonan was at work and Aunt Mary was cleaning and making stuffing. And, of course, listening for a phone call from Uncle Mike.

"That'll be a lot of kids under one roof," Dad said the night before.

"But my goodness, what that family's been through," Mom said. The fire in Nevada was under control, but another one was threatening a ski resort back in California. A couple of firefighters had been hurt, it said on the news. Uncle Mike was probably okay, but they hadn't heard from him for three days. Every morning, Aunt Mary marched across the park to the church. In her gray wool coat she looked very small and straight. Even from my attic window, I could see she was being brave. At Mack's, we got KitKats for me and Byron. Polly got a Milky Way. Byron's brother, Tom, was at hockey practice. I looked out Mack's window. Still sunny.

"We don't have a blizzard every Thanksgiving," said Mack, since this was only my second winter and we did last year. "But watch out for Easter." He winked and pretended to try to pound Polly's hand when she put the money down. She squeaked and pounded his hand.

We went up to my room and played with Pancake. Polly played with the twins. Then we dropped action figures down the laundry chute and threw a toy hippo for Dante. Then it was time for hockey practice. The girls in their new fuzzy suits — fake leopard skin and fake tiger, special delivery from Savanna — sat in their car seats. Polly sat between them. Mom had to call Dad at work twice, but she finally got the seats in the way back to pop up so Byron and I could sit there, with our hockey stuff. It was cool.

We didn't have a game over the weekend. Mrs. Almonio made us do a lot of stops and turns and skate backwards, which was boring for everyone except me. Then she let us have a long skating-around time.

"Mrs. Almonio?" Ryan raised his hand. "When will Mike Noonan be back?"

She looked at Byron, who skated away. We scrimmaged at the end. I fell down a couple more times, apologized, got told not to apologize, and sat on the bench.

"Is everything okay with the Noonans?" Mrs. Almonio asked me.

"Mike is working on another fire, and they haven't heard from him for a while," I said.

"And it's Thanksgiving," said Mrs. Almonio, shaking her head.

Clara's grandmother drove us back to our

house. "Any news?" she asked. Byron buttoned up his lower lip and shook his head. Clara looked back from the front seat. "He says no," she said. "And it's Thanksgiving," said her grandmother.

"We're having an early dinner, before your mother picks you up," said Mom. "I always think spaghetti's a good thing to have the day before Thanksgiving."

"No, thank you, Mrs. MacDougal-MacDuff," said Byron, "I'll wait in Morgy's room."

He went up the back stairs. My door slammed. Dante stuck his ears up. Pancake ran down. I started to get up from the table.

"He's upset about Uncle Mike," said Polly.

"Don't go up," said Mom. "He probably wants to be alone."

"He's probably crying," said Tom, who was back from his hockey practice. "Can I have his spaghetti?"

Byron's mom came over halfway through dinner. "You didn't have to do this," she said to Mom, and went up the back stairs to check on Byron. "He's got the door locked," she said.

"Sometimes it gets stuck," I said. You have to lift up the knob and lean on it. Byron was lying on my bed, looking at the bare, dead-looking branches of our old maple tree. "Sorry about the door," he said. He wasn't crying, he was frowning. He has black eyebrows. One goes up, the other goes down. "I hate how everyone wants him to be home for Thanksgiving, when he's *my* uncle."

"Yeah, I know," I said, although I didn't. Dante whined at the bottom of my stairs. It was time for his walk. "Okay, pretty soon," I told him.

"Plus, hockey just reminds me of him. Hockey *and* Thanksgiving."

"He was on duty last Thanksgiving," I said.

"Oh, yeah, that's right, he put out your chimney fire. But now he's all the way in California."

"I know," I said. "So's my aunt and my other friend, Keith. My aunt can't come because she spent so much money flying out here this summer. I might never see Keith again." Dante whined again. Now I was getting sad. The streetlights went on. Dark, scratchy branch shadows were on the wall of my room. "But the chimney didn't burn down, and your mom's here, and I bet Uncle Mike will call tomorrow, and my mom's making pies and we're coming to your house for dessert." I was trying to cheer myself up. I added, to myself, And I didn't get killed playing hockey, and Ferguson is not on our team, and Byron's still my friend. "And we play the trumpet," I said out loud.

Byron, still lying down, honked "let nothing you dismay!" on his trumpet.

"Boys? Are you all right?" said Mom.

"We're practicing," I said.

Dante whined again. Then there was a scramble, his long nose poked in my door, and he licked Byron.

"You like the trumpet, don't you, boy?" said Byron. "Cool dog."

It really was time for Dante's walk. He went down my stairs so fast he had to skid on the happy whale rug. Then he dived down to the front hall and landed in the boot pile. I gave Byron the leash so he could run down the front steps behind Dante. It was dark outside. Byron's mom had taken Polly and Tom home.

We went up to the top of the hill. We could see all the way to the turnpike. Cars were stuck in traffic on their way to Thanksgiving. I remembered the blizzard last Thanksgiving, when Mom and Dad were snowed out. I told Byron how I made this sort of promise that if they made it back I would try hockey and be a better friend to him, and less of a doof. He didn't say anything. Dante was tiptoeing after a squirrel. "So, right, then you came over, and

my parents did make it home for Thanksgiving." I said.

"Huh," said Byron. "You got what you wanted."

"Well, yeah, plus you came over and all."

"Even though you were still kind of doofy."

"Huh."

"Just kidding." We walked down the back of the hill by the old mansions. He didn't say anything. I made another promise, to keep remembering that Uncle Mike could learn what he needed to learn with or without flames, and not to worry about Byron. Then Byron said, "Okay. " He went up his porch steps. "I'm trying it. Let's see what happens."

Thanksgiving, it rained. We had our dinner at two, like the Noonans, so we would be on time with the pies. Mom said she was grateful for all of us, including the little girls who weren't here last year. Except in her tummy, I pointed out. Dad said he was grateful I was on the hockey team and wasn't practicing my trumpet too much. I said I was grateful for Dante. Dante was eating a turkey neck, which Bethany said would be good for his teeth. Phoebe and Penelope were having real sweet potatoes and stuffing, and turkey baby food. Pancake sat on the window seat licking his paws after kibbles with gravy.

It stopped raining, so we decided to walk to the Noonans'. Just as Mom got the girls in their stroller, with the pies stacked on the sunshade, and Dad and I got our coats on and shut the front door and we were all standing out on the porch, the phone rang.

"I wonder if that's Laura Noonan," said Mom. She unlocked the door and went back in but the phone stopped. She brought some cream in case it was Mrs. Noonan and that's what she wanted, put the cream on top of the pies, and locked the door. Dad put the pies on the steps, handed me the cream, picked up the stroller, and carried it down.

"You girls are so heavy," he grunted. They thought that was funny. The phone rang again. Mom unlocked the door and it stopped. She called Mrs. Noonan, but the line was busy. So she gave me a pie to carry, took one herself, and we went uphill behind Dad, who was running with the stroller, going "Wheee!" with the girls screaming. The clouds were dark gray and light gray, going fast, the leaves on the sidewalk were like wet cereal left in a bowl, and the tree trunks were shiny.

"It feels like snow," Mom said.

"Or worse," Dad said.

But when Aunt Mary opened the door, warm air

and turkey smells swarmed out on the porch. Aunt Mary was laughing. The phone was ringing.

"That'll be for you, dear," she said to Mom, taking the pies into the kitchen.

Mom got the phone off the little table in the crook of the staircase.

"Well, hello! How did you know we —? Oh! Oh, my goodness. He did?" She sat down on the bottom stair and listened. She talked and talked in a quiet voice. She seemed very interested. Dad put the girls on the floor to unsnap their fuzzy suits, but they crawled away, dragging them. Byron, Polly, Tom, Mr. and Mrs. Noonan, and Franky, a firefighter friend of Uncle Mike's, were sitting around the dining room table. The chandelier sparkled. The table was huge, with a lace cloth, and, in the middle, candles, chrysanthemums, and a turkey made out of a pine cone, pipe cleaners, and leaves. Aunt Mary passed out pie plates. Mrs. Noonan poured coffee. I handed her the cream.

"Aw, she knew I needed cream," she said, and gave me a little hug.

Mr. Noonan smiled and folded his hands. "Here we all are again, thank God for that," he said. Aunt Mary put a pie on the table. Dad had both girls in his lap. I took a piece of pie to Mom, who went on talking.

"It worked," Byron said to me.

"What?" I said.

"Well," said Aunt Mary, "we got a call from Uncle Mike, who is fine. The fire is one hundred percent contained and the firefighters even had a special Thanksgiving dinner up there in a ski lodge, put on by some flight attendants who were there for the weekend."

"And he's coming home," said Byron. "Maybe in time for the next game."

"Whoa!" I said. I was so happy. Uncle Mike survived. Plus, I was sure he'd keep me on the bench. Aunt Mary said he was trapped for just a few hours when a tree fell across a canyon, but he figured out how the burn-over shelters worked and then found a way out of there, and everyone in his crew was safe and they never lost radio contact.

"I'll tell the rest," said Mom, coming to the table. Aunt Mary patted her lips with a white napkin, smiling.

"That was Aunt Savanna on the phone," said Mom. "She has some friends who are flight attendants. Sometimes they get together at Thanksgiving. They're her friends from that time she went to London without her suitcase, or was it the time she got on the wrong charter and went to Moscow? They had Thanksgiving on the beach once." Tom laughed. Aunt Savanna cracks him up. "So, these flight attendants made Thanksgiving dinner for the firefighters. They have their own cabin at High Pines. They had Thanksgiving yesterday, because some guys were flying home today, and some had family right around there they could go to. Anyway, Savanna was serving sweet potatoes, and someone tapped her on the shoulder. It was Uncle Mike."

"So they had Thanksgiving together," said Aunt Mary. "Well, not exactly together, because your aunt was on duty, serving dinner."

"And they want to have every Thanksgiving together," said Mom.

"So they're getting married!" said Byron's mom.

I didn't know what to say, so I ate some pie. But I couldn't taste anything. I put my fork down. "We're cousins," Byron said.

"Cousins-to-be," said Mom. "The wedding's in April."

We finished both pies. The sun came out and set. The girls crawled under the table with Polly. Dad wanted to know if Aunt Savanna had cooked anything. Mom said she didn't think so, but at least there were plenty of firefighters around. Mom told the story about Aunt Savanna's Crock-Pot blowing up and Dad told about Aunt Savanna's mountain bike going out of control just when the polo team was having a run and they saved her and she became their mascot. Tom laughed and laughed, but not Aunt Mary. Then the girls pulled the tablecloth so hard the ice water sloshed, so we cleared the dishes. Aunt Mary came out to the kitchen to tell us not to put the good glasses in the dishwasher. She put on her gray coat.

"Are you going to church?" I said.

"Just for a moment," she said, and went out the back door.

"But Uncle Mike is fine," Byron said. The door slammed. I watched her march across the park. "Now she has to pray about Aunt Savanna," I said.

SEVEN
Merry Gentlemen

LOCAL HERO HELPS HALT WESTERN WILDFIRES: WATCH OUT WOLVERINES.

Lt. Michael P. Noonan was back on duty Monday at the Puckett Corner Fire Department, after spending six weeks fighting record-breaking wildfires in California and Nevada. Noonan coaches the Puckett Corner Pumas, set to play their arch-rivals, the Mt. Auburn Wolverines, at the Puckett Corner Arena Saturday.

Dear Keith,

This guy is Byron's uncle, so, guess what? I do get to come out for spring break, since he's marrying Savanna! And we're coming to the wedding! If I live through this game. Can we play Collision Zone on your computer? See you, really,

Morgy

At hockey, when Mrs. Almonio gave Uncle Mike the clipboard, she hugged him. So did some mothers from last year's seven-and-unders. One brought him cookies. This year's seven-and-unders' coach got everyone clapping when Uncle Mike came onto the ice. The Pumas were cheering. The seven-and-unders came out of the locker room and yelled. Uncle Mike just put his hand on top of Byron's helmet and looked at the ice till it stopped.

When the seven-and-unders and moms left, he looked at the clipboard and said, "So, Mrs. Almonio drilled you."

Ryan booed and had to sit in the penalty box.

We did the drills Mrs. Almonio gave us, and worse ones. Backward crossovers, which look really cool when Byron and Kyril do it but I fall right down. And slides. And making the puck go up in the air. Clara could do that. We had to stop and start faster, zip around cones, and stay in control of the puck, all afternoon. Everyone was happy. I tried getting up faster when I fell. Uncle Mike noticed and said, "There you go."

In trumpet, we had gotten to "O-oh tidings of comfort and joy, comfort and joy." It still hadn't snowed.

"Friday, come to band practice," said Mr. Profundo. "The Senior Center Sing-Along is next week. They need you guys, bad."

"Yes!" said Byron Friday afternoon on the way to the music room. We were skipping the long-division bee. The band had three kids on flute, a cellist, some violinists, and three drummers. I didn't notice Clara till she stood up to play the flute solo in "Silent Night." Forget it, she can do everything. She made no mistakes and sat down with her serious face that no one would ever laugh at. Miss Vermeil wiped her eyes.

"See how she takes her time?" she said. "Okay, excuse me? Excuse me? If you have enough energy for that back there, I think we'll go right to 'God Rest Ye.'" It took a couple of tries for us to play at the same time as the band, but Miss Vermeil said, "Mr. Profundo has worked wonders. Now everyone try to sound like there are more of you." She showed us how to put our trumpets politely on our knees when we weren't playing in a song.

We trumpeted loud on the way home. Dogs barked. "Excellent," said Byron.

Mom was talking on the phone with my grandmother about Savanna and Uncle Mike's wedding, whether they would get married at the old Wentworth mansion that burned down but has romantic gardens, or the cute little chapel in Los Conejitos that Grammy likes much better, and it has a roof. Phoebe was giving Dante Cheerios from her high chair. Penelope was in the downstairs playpen rocking on all fours so it would lurch across the dining room. Mom made a walking sign with her hand and pointed to Dante. We ran down the front steps. It was getting colder. There was ice along the edges of the river. Igor trotted up wearing a blue fleece.

"It's really just a sweater," Bethany said. "He doesn't need a coat yet. But soon, they both will. Greyhounds originally came from ancient Egypt, where they didn't have our winters." Dante was just in his black fur, jogging along sniffing things.

We crossed Puckett Corner Bridge. The wind was colder there. The sky was dark gray, like just before that blizzard last year. The river was even darker. I put my hand on Dante's neck while we waited for the traffic light to change. "He's shivering," I said.

"I'll call Give a Hound a Home," said Bethany. "Maybe they have a loaner coat, till you can order him one."

"That would probably be good," I said. "My mother is pretty busy these days."

"Well, with the wedding coming up. Did you see Mike Noonan in the paper?"

"People who don't have kids on our team even come to practice."

"He means a lot to Puckett Corner. The Noonans are a special family. And you're almost one of them."

"Yeah," I said. "I guess." I would be the branch of the family that didn't save anyone or play hockey very well.

"Sure," she said, as if she could tell what I was thinking. "You can be the one that rescues greyhounds." Igor towed her down the river path and toward their house. I ran all the way home with Dante, in case he was cold.

Hockey practice was even harder that afternoon. It was all about passing. Sometimes I got the puck to Stan, but when he hit it to me, I had to stop skating to hit it back.

"Hustle," Uncle Mike said. "Picture Wolverines all around."

I was trying not to. Next time Stan hit it to me, Kyril skated by really close, and the puck just stuck to his stick and went with him. He swooped around behind the goal, then, *bam,* it was in the goal. If he was on the other team, he would be scary. Uncle Mike asked me if I knew I could skate behind the goal. I was probably scary, being on our team.

He drew a diagram on his white board and told us about breakouts. That's when you get the puck out from behind your own goal before the other team can shoot it in. Everyone else knew all about it. "What's the rule for breakouts?"

"Don't pass in front of the net!" they yelled.

We practiced breakouts. I was all hot. I couldn't keep the puck away from anyone but Uncle Mike, when he demonstrated how to do it.

At last he said, "Getting there, guys and Clara. Game tomorrow. Two o'clock. Come early." Kyril cut in front of me to get off the rink. I fell over. My skates made a scratchy noise as I tried to get up, like seven-and-unders skating fast. I felt tired and stupid. Uncle Mike gave me a little knock on the helmet. "Sometimes the one that's falling the most is the one that's learning the most." I got up. "There you go," he said. "Just hustle wherever you are. You can even hustle on the bench." That sounded good.

Saturday, I hustled on the bench. I watched the play. I cheered for people by name, but I didn't yell if Uncle Mike was yelling. I wiggled my toes in my skates, to keep moving and just check if they were still there. I didn't yawn or shiver too hard. The Wolverines were winning by two. "They usually destroy us," said Byron's dad behind me to Clara's grandmother, who was sewing fluffy ballerina fabric. "Having Mike back is psyching them out." I listened to Uncle Mike during the break.

The third period started. "Okay." Uncle Mike sat down next to me. "See the big guy in their front line?" He was like two Fergusons. He could even get the puck away from Kyril. "He's not paying any attention to Don over there. Does he have to? He should. And to you and Stan. He's going to think you're not as good as Kyril and Don, and that's where he'll be making a mistake." The mistake would be sending me in, I thought. *"Because,"* said Uncle Mike, "you'll be thinking harder than him. You and Stan get it away, and get it up to Clara, just once, okay?"

"Wait," I said, but he was already blowing his whistle and giving me a little shove, and my skates were sliding on the white cut-up ice. Out on the ice, Kyril looked at Uncle Mike and me and said, "Me?" Uncle Mike held the little gate to the bench open for him and Don to come off. The ref dropped the puck, the Wolverines clacked it, smacked it, and it clattered to me. This Wolverine was so big, he had to bend down to get in my way. I hit it to Stan. Stan hit it to Byron. Wolverines got it and sent it back to me. Then they were all around me. What did Uncle Mike tell me? Picture Wolverines all around, I told myself, as I fell.

They got a goal. It was my fault. I looked through the red and black Wolverine legs jumping up and down. Uncle Mike didn't pull me out. He held up his finger. "Just once." I got up. After the face-off, the puck sailed right to our goal. Ryan flopped over on his side and shoved it to me. Wolverines were all around, again. I took a breath. I didn't stop. I hit it and kept moving. It was as slow as a golf putt. But there I was, still standing so Stan could hit it to me and I could hit it to Clara. Anthony scooped it into the goal. Uncle Mike blew his whistle.

Kyril went back in and made a goal. "Nice," Uncle Mike said when I sat down. We tied. Kyril and Don looked at me like they were thinking what I was thinking: if they had stayed in, we could have won. "We play them again," said Uncle Mike.

On the way home, Byron's dad said, "Another assist, Morgy."

"Sorry I fell," I said when I got out of the van.

Mr. Noonan said, "Now I'm looking for your first goal." He was way too nice.

"Getting there," said Byron, also too nice, as he slid the van door closed.

At home, Dad was giving the girls a bath. Mom and Pancake were asleep on the couch. On the stair landing, there was a package from Give a Hound a Home. It was a greyhound coat. A bright red greyhound coat with white fluff on the inside.

"Whoa, Dante, check it out," I said. I slid it over his head and buckled the straps under his stomach. He looked silly, as if he was dressed up as Santa or a reindeer. He backed up and barked. He sat down and scratched. He stood up and shook.

"What?" said Mom, waking up.

"He needed a coat," I said, "so Bethany called Give a Hound a Home." Dante looked at her, tried to scratch his stomach standing up, and whined.

"Oh, how nice," said Mom, turning back the collar so he had a white ruff, even more Santa-like. "We'll have to send them a donation."

"Yark!" said Dante, and shook, from nose to whippy tail tip, to shake it off.

"He likes it," said Mom, "because he's so handsome in it." She patted behind his ears. "You are," she said, in the same voice she uses when she's trying to keep the girls from getting out of the stroller. "Red is your color."

He smiled.

"It matches your snow pants," said Dad. "Look at that face!" I have these awful snow pants. "Nancy, make this boy a hot dog and I'll take Dante out to show off his coat."

"Could I please have two hot dogs?" I was just starving, as if I had played the whole game.

"It keeps looking like snow," I said.

"But never snowing," said Byron. We were in the back of the bus on the way to the Senior Center Sing-Along on the last day of school before vacation. The sky was dark as ever. Outside it looked like a black-and-white TV show. Leaves herded across the road. The bus stopped for runaway garbage cans. We had on white shirts and black clip-on ties. We were missing our class parties, but Miss Vermeil said the senior citizens would take care of us.

The bus climbed to the top of the hill, then joggled down an old driveway. The Senior Center was an old house with a big wide porch made of stones. In the window, it said *Happy Holidays* in red tinsel letters.

Aunt Mary, with a miniature knitted Christmas stocking pinned on her jacket, opened the door. "Just in time. I put the music stands in front of the fireplace." She straightened Byron's tie, licked her thumb and got his hair to all go the same way. "Handsome is as handsome does. Oh, feel that wind. That's bringing the snow."

As if she had said a magic word, snow started to fall, thickly and all at once. I looked up from putting my music on my stand. The Puckett Corner senior bus was here, already getting covered in snow. The seniors got out, hunching their shoulders. "Meemo meemo meeemo" went the chorus, warming up their voices, while the seniors from the bus stomped their boots in the hall and came in looking for radiators to put their scarves on. More seniors parked their cars on the lawn.

Miss Vermeil let the drummers play "Pa-Rumpa-Pum-Pum" as background music while the seniors found their seats. Some went back and got their coats. Some went out on the porch to look at the sky. The lights went out. "Oh, for goodness sakes," said a lady, and she stood up to leave. "Puckett Electric is sending a truck," Aunt Mary said. The lady sat down. "And now . . ." She held out her hand. Miss Vermeil tapped her stand.

The band was too quiet. They played "The Dreidel Song" and "Jingle Bells" as if they were tuning up. But on "Silent Night," Clara did great. Her music fell off her stand and she kept playing. Everyone stopped checking their watches and the snow and kept their eyes on Clara, as if they could help her remember the notes. Of course, she knew it by heart. She nods while she plays, maybe to pump out the air, and her hair goes forward.

I like to watch her, but I couldn't because outside I saw a commotion in the snow. Somehow I was afraid it might be Mom, and it was. Mom, running behind the double stroller with the girls under a blanket and Dante romping ahead of them in his red and white coat. He liked the snow. He jumped around in a circle and snapped at it.

Then it was time for Byron and me to play our song. Just as we started to trumpet "God Rest Ye Merry, Gentlemen," I saw Dante run past the picture window with his leash flying out straight behind him. Mom was not holding it. Miss Vermeil was raising her hands to us, as if to say, "Louder!" Dante ran back and forth in front of the Senior Center, wagging and sniffing. Mom ran after him, missing the leash. Penelope bounced up and down. The stroller's sunshade was filled with snow. Dante's black rump disappeared into the woods. Penelope reached up. All the snow in the sunshade fell on the girls. They began to cry. Mom stopped chasing Dante and flopped her arms down at her sides.

Byron thought of the same thing at the same time as me, on the last "O-oh tidings of comfort and joy." It's supposed to end, Miss Vermeil had said, "if not quietly, at least sweetly." We both stood up and trumpeted as loud as we could. Miss Vermeil blinked. A lady who had wiped her eyes during "Silent Night" put her hanky over her

mouth. Dante stopped in the woods and pointed his ears.

We played it again, "O-oh ti-i-dings of comfort and joyyyyy," really long at the end, really loud and corny. The chorus was staring at us. The rest of the band put their instruments politely on their knees. A thin man with a sharp nose and a gray scarf stood up and said, "Encore!" and clapped. We played it again, with the man in the scarf clapping and stamping his galoshes and the other seniors singing along. I couldn't see Dante anymore. I tried to play louder than everyone so he'd hear me and come, and not run down the hill into traffic.

It was the last "comfort and joy." I played as loud as I could. I didn't see Dante. Everyone was laughing and clapping. Mom came in from the coatroom, looking sorry. I was out of breath. Bang! A door slammed. Dante ran in from the kitchen in his red coat, with snow on his head, through the seniors, the chorus, past Miss Vermeil and the rest of the band, and licked Byron and me.

"Must be Santa!" Miss Vermeil yelled. The chorus sang and the seniors laughed. I took off Dante's coat. Byron helped Aunt Mary pour the punch.

Other kids helped ladies put out plates and plates of cookies.

"Nice work," said the man with the gray scarf. "Did my heart good. Here, may I see that?" He took my trumpet and looked it over. He wiped off the mouthpiece. "Do you mind?" he asked, then made it go "Broot, trrroot!" in a cool way. "No," he said, "It's not the trumpet, it's you."

Penelope had a coconut snowman. Phoebe let a lady wipe her tears. "I wanted to hear my son play," Mom was saying. "They'll sit still after a stroller ride, and it was time for the dog's walk, so we all came. I'm sorry," she said to Aunt Mary, "I thought we could just stand at the back."

"Oh, now, what fun would that have been?" Aunt Mary said, and gave her a hug.

Dante ate a candy cane with the wrapper on. A lady stroked him and he turned around and smiled at her. "Whoo!" she said, and clapped. Someone lit a fire in the fireplace. The man with the scarf was playing "Let It Snow, Let It Snow, Let It Snow" on my trumpet. People were laughing.

Our bus started up. In the Senior Center, they were dancing. "Have Yourself a Merry Little

Christmas" went my trumpet. I stood by the fireplace eating a mini Yule log and waiting to get it back. Miss Vermeil pulled me out the door. The snowflakes were dark gray in front of the fire-lit window. She said, "Don't worry, Mr. Profundo will get your trumpet back, " as we got on the bus.

"Whoa," said Byron as we watched Mom, Dante, and the girls glide down the path toward home, "cool dog coat."

EIGHT
Wolverines, Again

Hey, Morgy, Wow, you'll be here soon. Did I tell you I got Collision Zone III? You'll like it. Have to go practice, we have a spring concert. Which kills! See you soon, really soon! Keith

I couldn't believe I was going back to California. I would see Keith. Byron would see Keith. I could play with my old soccer team, on grass. I hadn't seen green grass in Puckett Corner since Christmas. I especially couldn't believe it because before we left, we had another Mr. Hansom project: "Make a board game about someone in history." Byron and I had Thomas A. Edison. We couldn't even get the light bulb to light. Not only that, I also had to live through another hockey game. The second Wolverines game, in fact, on their rink, at Mt. Auburn Academy.

We were in the dining room. Big snowflakes fell past bare gray trees. Mom was on the phone. The baby gate was across the bottom of the stairs and Phoebe and Penelope were crawling around. Pancake jumped on a dust bunny and ran away from it sideways, pretending it was after him. Penelope reached for his tail. He jumped lightly up through the banisters and sat on the fourth stair with his tail behind him. Dante watched with his chin on a large purple bunny.

"Maybe it's a bad bulb," said Byron, shaking it.

"We should have done Alexander Graham Bell," I said.

Byron screwed the light bulb back in, again. This time it went on.

"Okay!" I said. The light was the most important thing. We also had a model train on the board. That was because when he was a kid, Thomas Edison sold candy on the train. He had a lab in the baggage car so he could do experiments in his spare time. Byron drew an arrow pointing to the lab with a marker. We also had his grownup lab, made out of a baby wipes box. The game was to roll the dice and jump the game pieces around to visit his house, the labs, and his inventions. I glued on the light switch.

We still had to make the inventions and write Edison facts on the game cards. But it looked pretty good. It looked very good. We went and had a snack. There was a crash. Penelope was standing up, holding the corner of the table. The game was on the floor. Phoebe was sitting next to it, reaching for the train.

"Noooo!" We ran in. The girls cried. Mom picked up Penelope. I put Phoebe in her playpen. "Eeeee," they went. Dante jumped up and looked around. Pancake ran upstairs.

"She wants the train," said Mom. Penelope was leaning out of Mom's arms, reaching for the train and yelling. I ran up to the bathroom and got the squeezy locomotive, but Penelope batted it out of my hand. "Uh, wahh!"

Byron unhooked the caboose and gave it to her. She put a corner of it in her mouth. I picked up the game.

"Great," I said to Mom. "We were supposed to finish today! Look, it's wrecked." The lab had come unstuck and the light bulb was broken, also the dog that listens to the gramophone and hears his master's voice. Mom let us have the light bulb from her sewing machine and said we could use Dad's label maker. Then Clara's grandmother beeped for hockey practice.

"Don't let her take the caboose in the bath," I said. Penelope liked to hold her squeezy locomotive underwater so it bubbled, but they both liked my stuff better.

"At least they can't get up your stairs," said Byron.

"Yet," I said. They could crawl really fast and grab stuff and put it in their mouths, but they were still little, so you had to let Mom take it away from them.

Hockey was all about strategy. Uncle Mike said that since we were smaller than the Wolverines, we had to be smarter. We practiced skating left but passing to the right. He thought this would be especially good for "thinkers, like Morgy here."

He made us go faster. We got tired. He took out the white board. He drew Wolverines, which were O's, surrounding us, X's, and ways out. Then he pretended to be a Wolverine and made us keep the puck away from him. "As long as you shoot to a Puma, the puck can even go backwards." But then I shot one into our goal. "Up to a point," he added. And I'm the thinker? I thought.

At skating-around time, Kyril was doing backwards crossovers, fast. He crashed into me. I fell down so hard I couldn't breathe. Kids looked down at me. I looked up at them. Finally, I gasped. Uncle Mike helped me up. "Skate slowly around the rink, then sit down for a minute," he said. "Do you have something to say, Kyril?"

"Watch out," said Kyril. Uncle Mike said this was no-check hockey, and even if I were a Wolverine, Kyril would have to apologize. "Him, a Wolverine?" Kyril said, and laughed rudely. Then, whenever he skated near me, he went, "Oh-oh, the thinker," and swerved away, backwards.

At last we could go home. "Tomorrow the game's at four," said Uncle Mike. "Be early. Don, you're leaving early for Disney World, right? So Morgy, you and Stan will take turns in the line with Kyril." After practice, Kyril was talking to Uncle Mike. He looked at me, then skated away looking mad. I knew what he meant. I was bad enough in Stan's line. Dad picked up me, Byron, and Clara. We dropped Clara off and went right home. Byron started making labels. I wiped some banana off the caboose, found the gramophone, and glued the dog back together. It looked better. Byron's mom called and said he had to come home and try on his cousins' blazers, for the wedding.

"I'll stick on the labels," I said. I took the label maker and punched out "Thomas A. Edison's Excellent Invention Tour." "Excellent?" I put my head down on the table and pretended I was small enough to get on the train. I could see the pencil marks that the marker didn't cover. Thomas Edison's lab looked like a baby wipes box. I couldn't play hockey. Kyril hated me. Nothing was excellent.

"I guess we're still eating in the kitchen because of the boys' project," Mom said. "Oh, Morgy, I didn't see you in there." The swinging door shut. I heard her taking tuna noodle casserole out of the oven.

"Could you call Mike Noonan and ask him not to play me?" I said at dinner.

"I could," said Dad, "but he's the coach. He has to decide. What's wrong?" But then the phone rang. "It's Savanna," Dad said. "Your green sandals came and they look nice." Penelope reached over and put chocolate pudding on Phoebe's head. Phoebe screamed. "That's it. Bath time!" Mom said. She grabbed Phoebe out of the high chair and ran upstairs. "You bring that one!" Dad took Penelope.

I picked up the phone. "What's going on out there?" said Savanna.

"Penelope put pudding on Phoebe's head," I said.

"Morgo?" said Savanna. "Is that you? It doesn't sound like you."

"Well, maybe it's because I got the wind knocked out of me in hockey."

"No, that wouldn't do it. In Brownies, I thought I could jump right off the swings and into the ocean. Of course, I hit the beach and everyone laughed. You get your voice right back as soon as you can breathe. You just sound sad, Morgo."

Everything happens to Savanna, and she gets over it. She makes me feel like a baby. I asked her to tell Uncle Mike not to play me tomorrow. She said okay, and I said he probably wouldn't listen. He would talk me into it. I would fall and Kyril would hate me. She asked what I was afraid of, Kyril or falling? And I said, "Kyril. I'm used to falling." She said, "Aw, Morgo," and sang me a song from her favorite movie. "Pick yourself up, dust yourself off, and start all over again." Savanna is someone who doesn't mind singing on the phone.

"Are you crying?" she said.

"No." I was just listening, thinking of all the times I ever fell down, in my whole life.

"Oh, that's right, you're big now. I'll call Mike. I think you need a big hug."

"Or an earlier flight to Los Angeles." Then we laughed, or Savanna did, and I wiped my nose, and Mom and Dad came back downstairs. We had dessert and I went to bed. Outside was an ice storm. The tree in my window was shiny all over. The rain rattled. I wondered why I ever thought I could play hockey, or belonged here.

The next day, Aunt Mary was driving us to the Wolverines game, so I went home with Byron. His cousins' blazers were all over his room. Polly was wearing another cousin's flouncy dress and walking up and down the hall listening to her party shoes tap. Aunt Mary made me try on a blazer. It belonged to David or Danny Noonan and it was part of a private school uniform, with golden buttons and a crest on the pocket. Byron had one, too. The door opened downstairs. "It's the groom," said Aunt Mary, looking over the banister.

"Wow," said Uncle Mike, coming up. "Now I guess I'll have to get dressed up, too, just to keep up with Polly. Morgy, can I talk to you a minute?"

I went out in the hall in David or Danny's blazer. I never should have told Aunt Savanna to call him. He was already being too nice to me, plus, he was getting married.

"It's tough bringing up your skills when you're playing in games. But I wish you'd play. We need you. Kyril's fast, but he doesn't always think before he shoots. You're thinking all the time. You guys together in a line could be great."

"Except he hates me," I said.

"No, he's just impatient. Give him a break. He just moved here from Russia. Hockey's probably all he can do right now. Just came in October or something."

That was when I came, last year. It's terrible being new when the school year has already started. But I didn't go around knocking people over.

"I guess," I said.

"Great! And one other little thing. Ask your aunt if I could lose the cummerbund?"

"The what?"

"It's a sash thingy I'm supposed to wear. Dyed the color of your mother's shoes." He looked a little upset.

"Okay."

"And don't worry. I'll pull you out if it gets bad. You should wear that. It fits."

But I always thought it got bad way before he did.

Aunt Mary drove us to Mt. Auburn Academy. She said we could have the game out in the parking lot. She had on her ice-gripper boots, which have little metal claws on the bottom to keep her from slipping. Byron and Clara skated around in their snow boots. I fell. Aunt Mary stuck out her elbow. It was thin but felt like iron. I wished she would come out on the rink so I could hang on when I felt that falling feeling. She patted my mitten when we got to the rink so I would let go. "Nothing to fear but fear itself!" she said, and winked.

It was like putting on a wet bathing suit to go swimming. I couldn't stop shivering. Byron and Clara looked serious but normal. In skating-around time, Clara made a lot of goals and Byron practiced changing directions. Kyril zipped around the edges of the rink, making fast, scraping turns and not looking at me. Sitting on the bench with my stomach jumping, I thought how Uncle Mike wasn't scared of tall flames, but of a green cummerbund, and how Kyril wasn't scared of Wolverines, but of our school, maybe. I used to be afraid of our school, too, when I was new. And recess, and Ferguson knocking me over, and people laughing at me.

In the first quarter, Stan was with Kyril. He was good. Like Uncle Mike said, the Wolverines didn't know to watch out for Stan. They surrounded Kyril because they had to, but Stan could get the puck away from them. He got a goal.

"Okay," said Uncle Mike. "Now they start to get it, so now the thinker goes in. Just to shake them up."

To shake me up. Almost before Stan sat down in my place on the bench, the puck was flying at me. Kyril got it, faked that he was passing to me, and hit it to Ryan, who airlifted it to Clara. Wolverines got it away and it came back. I was surrounded, with the puck stuck behind my stick. I couldn't fake a pass or even pass for real. I couldn't move. A Wolverine hit my stick, hard. There was no room to fall down even, but they got the puck away. But Ryan hit it away from our goal. Then Kyril was surrounded.

See how he likes it, I thought. Then I thought, He's a new kid. What could I do for a new kid? When I was surrounded, I needed someone behind me. So I skated around behind Kyril. He nudged it to me. I hit it to Clara. Anthony and Byron made a goal.

After that, the big Wolverine from the last game hung around me, keeping the puck away, so no Wolverines came near me either. I wasn't even scared, just bored. Kyril did all the work. Then he messed up. He just hit it. No one was there to get it. It was all alone on the ice. Everyone went after it, even the guy guarding me. I stood around with Ryan by the goal. The Wolverines did get it, so it came shooting down the ice. Everyone from both teams was clacking and clattering behind it, like a train coming. Then I thought, That wouldn't have mattered to Thomas Edison. He could invent stuff in a baggage car.

There was all this space around the puck. I skated toward everyone and hit it really hard, since I was about to be knocked over. It bounced off the side of the rink, behind them. They all went after it, but Clara was waiting for it. She made a goal.

I looked at Uncle Mike, but he didn't take me out. The rest of the game didn't last very long. I fell a couple times, but Kyril got the puck. Byron made two goals. We won.

"Nice," said Uncle Mike.

"Whoa," said Byron.

"Huh," I said, slapping hands with Wolverines as we went through the line. The weird thing was, it was no big deal. I mean, everyone clapped and stuff, but it turned out winning wasn't that different from losing. I fell down just as much, but I did two things right, instead of zero things right.

"He is the thinker," said Kyril, socking me on the back.

NINE
Savanna's Day

Hey, Keith, maybe I'll see you before you read this. Morgy.

"Whoa! Palm trees?" said Byron as the plane bumped and squeaked onto the runway.

At the gate, Grammy was hopping up and down with her umbrella up, she was so glad to see us. "And these are the new little girls!" she said. Penelope blew a raspberry. Grammy blew one on Penelope's neck. "Oh, I love that baby smell! And Morgy is tall now, and you must be Byron." You could just walk out of the airport and smell trees and flowers and step on the sidewalk, with no ice. Mom said, "Back in your habitat, puppy dog!" and put my snow jacket in her bag.

We had to go to the wedding rehearsal, so we couldn't see Keith yet. Los Conejitos is up a winding road behind Grammy's house, just the other side of the first row of mountains. In the spring, a creek flows right across the road. The church had brown shingles all over it and flowers creeping up it and fancy, curly carved wood around the edges.

"It's such a cute church," said Mom in the car. "And it's a good thing she isn't getting married at the Wentworth place. I'm sure we'll all be glad to have a roof over our heads."

Mr. White, the minister, let me and Byron sit in the balcony. The organist played and everyone practiced walking up the aisle. Flowers were everywhere, and white bows. Tom walked with Mom. Then came Savanna's friend Sky and Franky from the Puckett Corner Fire Department. After them Polly, tapping in her party shoes, and behind her a big space for Savanna's kindergarten art students. They were coming up from Los Angeles tomorrow for the wedding, in their own bus. Then came Dad with Savanna. They kept having to start over. Only Polly had the walk right. Byron and I listened to the rain on the roof and played Tom's old Game Boy.

"Soon," I said, "we'll be playing Collision Zone III at Keith's."

On the way home, a branch bobbed across the road in the creek.

"Those little white marks way up on the mountainside are waterfalls," said Mom. "You don't see those every spring. Can you see the black part where the fire was?" Rain hammered on the car roof. The mountaintops were in clouds.

At Grammy's we had pizza and watched TV while the grownups ate in the dining room. It was Phoebe and Penelope's first pizza. Even with Polly watching them, they wiped their hands on the curtains behind their high chairs. Rain rattled onto the patio like gray marbles. Palm leaves drooped to the ground. The Noonans all went to a motel, but Byron got to sleep over with me in Grammy's hide-a-bed couch.

A rumbling sound woke us up. First we thought it was an earthquake, but I remembered they don't last that long. We went outside to look. It was coming from behind the bushes at the end of

Grammy's lawn, behind the little cupid statue, behind the fence. It was Rock Creek, full to the top. The rocks were crashing into each other.

In the kitchen, Grammy was talking on the phone. She was still in her bathrobe, with curlers and extra rows of frown lines. "So we don't have the flowers or the organ music, and even Savanna's veil is up there, but Mr. White was visiting an old lady in the hospital near here when the road went out, so he can still marry them," she was saying. "Well, thank you." She hung up. "That was your Aunt Mary. We've had a change of plans." She got us some strawberries. The phone rang again. She put bread in the toaster for us and said firmly, "It's no use trying to get up to the church, Savanna. I called the Highway Patrol. I got your friend Roger. His exact words were, 'No way, and tell Banana MacDoof to have a good one.' Can you imagine? Oh, now don't cry! You don't care about fifth grade anymore! Just come over with your cell phone so we can call everyone. The wedding will be right here in the house."

Savanna, crying? I reached for the phone. "You're crying?" I said.

"No," she sniffed.

I didn't say, "You are, too," because she didn't do

that to me. I said, "I didn't think so. Guess what, I was okay in hockey. I mean, I fell down, but Kyril doesn't hate me, and we won. And the Wolverines are huge."

"Hey, Morgo, excellent." She sniffled.

Grammy had the TV on. "Supposed to stop!" she said.

"Did you hear that? It's supposed to stop. Grammy saw it on TV."

"But they won't get the road fixed in time," said Savanna.

For someone who's always cheering people up, Savanna is pretty hard to cheer up herself. I couldn't think of anything else, so I just said, "One thing? Uncle Mike can't wear the cummerbund, okay?"

"You already call him Uncle Mike?" She blew her nose. "Well, how's a little rain going to change that? Just like Grammy always said, we're not made of sugar, we won't melt. Wait! I know. Ask Grammy if she could please meet me at the Wentworth Mansion. We need umbrellas and a boom box."

"Nonsense," said Grammy when I gave her the message. "It's all wet up there. We're having it here in the house." I told her that Savanna said that she,

Grammy, always said we're not made of sugar and we won't melt.

"Hmph," said Grammy. "That was about playing outside, not getting married."

Aunt Mary came in, folding up her plastic rain hat. "Should we rearrange the furniture for the marriage service?" she said. When Grammy told her about Savanna and the Wentworth Mansion, Aunt Mary made a little gasp, but she said, "It's her day."

"Well, if you know Savanna," said Grammy, "you know this is just her kind of day." Aunt Mary said she was beginning to see that, but she had to insist they would *not* be getting married with a boom box. She held up two black cases. Our trumpets. "Morgy's mother and I thought you'd like to hear the boys later, so I brought them. And their blazers match," she added.

So Grammy got on her raincoat and went up to the Wentworth Mansion with some garbage bags, "because you never know what you'll find up there." She said Dad could come up and help but we should practice our piece.

"Our piece?" said Byron, looking scared.

"That is the responsibility you accept when you

learn an instrument," said Aunt Mary. "Our gifts are not for us alone."

"'God Rest Ye'?" said Byron, looking scared.

"'Ode to Joy,'" I said. "Has to be." Byron looked more scared. We had only played that once with Mr. Profundo. "We'll play the part we know and go from there." I wasn't scared. I barely even had time to notice I wasn't. We started playing, like elephants clearing their throats, or trunks maybe.

"'Ode to Joy'? You're kidding, that's what we're working on," said a voice. First I thought, Oh, good, he can tell what it is. Then I thought, Keith!

"Yay!" I yelled. "You look the same!" Keith has curly hair, green eyes, dark brown skin, and curly eyebrows.

He said, "You're going to the wedding in your pajamas?" We got dressed. He went home and got his trumpet. In the kitchen, Aunt Mary was making scrambled eggs for Mom and Dad. Mom was calling wedding guests to tell them to go to the Wentworth Mansion. We tried to learn all of "Ode to Joy." Dad tried to help us on the piano, but then Savanna came in wearing jeans and said Grammy would like him to come up to the Wentworth Mansion and help. We had the first part. We were beginning to get the rest when Mr. White knocked on the door in his big minister robes. "Can my trumpeters follow me?" he said. Just then the doorbell rang.

"It's the kindergartners! My mother's going to kill me!" Savanna ran past us in the hallway. "Okay, one more project," she was saying to about twenty kids as we left.

Keith and I used to Rollerblade down the driveway of the Wentworth place. It's long and straight, and goes uphill between two rows of tall, thin trees that were flicking water. All that's left of the mansion is a flat place with fancy stone steps, banisters, and a huge view of the ocean, which today looked extra wet.

"I've never done a wedding at sea," said Mr. White, with rain on his glasses. He told us to stand quietly behind the banisters till we saw Savanna, then "play for all you're worth." I practiced pushing down the valves without blowing notes.

Cars began to park in the grass. Umbrellas bobbed up the driveway. Some people wore fancy shoes with leaves and grass stuck to them, some wore boots, and some went barefoot and carried their shoes. Other than that they just looked like regular dressed-up people. They stood around and waited. Uncle Mike and Byron's dad came and stood with Mr. White.

Grammy and Aunt Mary came in flowery dresses with rain hats and boots. I kept figuring out the song. Byron's mom pushed Phoebe and Penelope up in their stroller. Then came Tom, with Mom in her green dress and shoes, and Sky with Franky, and then a big gap. Everyone looked around. Here came Polly in front of a line of kids in yellow slickers. Polly just had on her fluffy dress. "She never gets cold," said Byron.

"Here we go," said Mr. White.

"What are you smiling at?" said Uncle Mike.

"Trumpeters?" Mr. White said. "Tra!" we started, just like stepping off a cliff. Byron and Keith looked at my hand to see what valves to push down. I just played.

There was Savanna, in her long white wedding dress, holding my dad's elbow. Trees dripped. Savanna was smiling. She had on the green cummerbund. Her veil was blowing out straight. It was made of white paper covered with little silver and gold handprints. The kindergartners, right in front of us, cheered. She arched her eyebrows and they stopped. Keith and Byron finished the part they knew and stopped. I kept going, loud. I thought of Dante, at home in Puckett Corner.

I think the wind that started was a good thing. It blew the clouds apart so there was blue sky right over the wedding. Also, it was so loud, probably no one heard me. They were all smiling. Uncle Mike took Savanna's hands with his coattails flapping.

Keith and Byron played the last part with me. Grammy put her foot on the veil so it would be quiet. Everyone stood close to hear Mr. White. Savanna said her vows slowly, as if she were teaching them to the kindergartners. Uncle Mike held her hands and talked calmly. It went fast. Just when Uncle Mike kissed Aunt Savanna, a whole bunch of guys in helmets, boots, and bright yellow shirts ran up the path. I thought it was an emergency but Byron said, "It's the crew from New Hampshire."

We played "God Rest Ye." The firefighters made two lines and held up big long axes to make an arch for them to run under.

"Pulaski trenching tools, remember?" Byron said. "For making firebreaks." One last puff of wind blew little white flowers off the trees onto Mike

127

and Savanna as they went down the driveway. Grammy and Aunt Mary held hands and wiped their eyes. Then everyone else started down the hill to Grammy's. We stopped playing. I was so glad it was over. My lips were still buzzing.

"That was very brave," said Aunt Mary, who had waited for us.

"More than brave," said Mr. White, folding Aunt Mary's hand over his arm. "A joyful noise."

When we got to Grammy's, the sun was out. There was all this food, and waiters, and even a band on the patio. Savanna and Mike shook hands with everyone. The guys carrying their shoes turned out to be the polo team. Roger from the highway patrol dropped by. A guy said to me, "I hear you got my greyhound," and gave me a thumbs up. He gave Savanna a big kiss. Then he borrowed an electric guitar and played with the band.

When the band took a break, everyone told Savanna stories. There was Thanksgiving on the beach, the exploding Crock-Pot, the bicycle and the polo team, and of course, the time she set our chimney on fire and met Uncle Mike. Tom laughed and laughed. Aunt Mary didn't seem to mind or even hear them. She and Grammy had taken off their shoes and were having tea on the couch. Polly and the Los Angeles kindergartners played Duck, Duck, Goose. Then Uncle Mike and Aunt Savanna cut the cake, and when everyone was still licking icing off their fingers, it started to rain again. Savanna's bouquet flew through the air to Sky.

"There they go," said Mom. I couldn't see them for a minute. Then there was a familiar peppery, flowery smell. I was being hugged harder than I had ever been hugged.

"Morgo! You played a solo! I love that song!" said Savanna.

"Ah-choo!" I said. And then they really did leave.

People started finding their shoes and thanking Grammy. Keith's mom talked to my mom. We got to go home with Keith to play Collision Zone III. Phoebe and Penelope were standing up to get cake off the table. A photographer took a picture of them in their pink dresses and hats. "Nap time," said Mom.

I thought I would be sad when the plane landed in Boston. Instead of palm trees there were close-together houses with surprised-eyebrow roofs over the top windows, gray streets, a dirty beach for boats, not surfers, and trees that were still mostly black. But I was happy. I got to see Keith and play soccer and Collision Zone III. Plus, Byron came. Plus, Byron lived here, and Pancake and Dante, and even Savanna was moving here, although she would have to commute for a few weeks to finish up with her L.A. kindergartners.

"They were good as gold," said Miss Merriweather, who looked after Pancake and Dante. "Clara came by every day to walk Dante." Pancake, sitting on the window seat, was extra fluffy, as if he'd been brushed. He smiled with his eyes closed. Penelope pulled herself up and reached for his tail. I picked him up, but just to be sure he was safe, he kicked off my chest and ran upstairs, fluffing out his tail as he passed Dante, who was racing down. Dante smiled, wagged and wagged, and skidded up the hall rug. Time for a walk.

At school, we got our projects back. "I especially liked the raccoon and gramophone," Mr. Hansom wrote on ours.

"I should have made a new dog instead of gluing the broken one together," I said.

"But we got an A minus," said Byron. One day, when we were choosing teams to play States and Capitals Baseball, Miss Vermeil, on the PA system, asked me and Byron to come to the music room, immediately.

"Do you think we're in trouble for taking the trumpets to California?" said Byron. I knew you weren't supposed to leave them in a parked car, but I couldn't remember if there were rules about traveling.

"Do you boys think you will continue in the program next year?" Miss Vermeil asked. Maybe we would be kicked out, I thought. Maybe we would just have to pay a fine, like with overdue books. Clara was there, too.

"Yes," I said. "Sure," said Byron.

"Well, good. Colonel Profundo's music camp awards one scholarship a year to the best music student. Clara Hagopian won it this year." Clara ducked her head in case we were even thinking about laughing. I was just thinking how she can do everything. "But the colonel has added a 'promising beginners' category. This year, it's for you boys. If you care to attend, you will be his guests."

"You mean, our trumpet teacher is a colonel?" said Byron.

"Oh, no." Miss Vermeil laughed. "The colonel is Mr. Profundo's grandfather. He's famous around here. You met him at the Senior Center Sing-Along. I think it was Morgy who loaned him his trumpet. He was quite impressed, Morgy, and with your technique, too."

"Cool," said Byron. "If it's not the same time as hockey camp."

"Can I fill out the form?" I said. "We have twins, a cat, and a greyhound, and sometimes things get lost."

Hey Morgy, I can't believe you got to come. It was excellent. Keith

Keith, thank your dad for driving us to practice. You should be goalie. I can't believe your sister has a hedgehog. Next time, you're coming here. Bring all the Collision Zones. Morgy.
P.S. Bring skates. Byron.